JURASSIC HELL

RUSS WATTS

SEVERED PRESS
HOBART TASMANIA

JURASSIC HELL

To the beautiful Yasawa Islands and Napoleon for inspiring me.

CHAPTER 1

They walked through the dense heat grateful that it would only be for a short time. The chief of the local tribe had given them two days to explore the unnamed island for the rover. Given that it was already approaching forty degrees and not even midday, they were all hoping that it wouldn't actually take two days to find it.

"Ricardo, what do you make of this?" asked Tobias stopping to pick up a tiny fragment of metal. It was barely bigger than his hand and the metal was blackened and charred. It was twisted as if it had been melted and reformed.

"Yeah, I'd say that's a piece of the outer hull. No doubt. We're on the right trail. Where was it?" Ricardo Mendez was the team leader. He was leading the merry expedition through the jungle in the hope of retrieving a very expensive piece of machinery. That was just the first step. The real gold was what that machinery contained.

"Over here by these vines." Tobias knelt and pointed to the thick vines covering the jungle floor. His back ached and sweat rolled down his forehead. "There. I can see another piece." He reached into the green jungle floor and plucked out another piece of metal.

"Let me see that." Ricardo knelt down beside Tobias and examined the lump of charred metal. "We're close."

"Thank the Lord for that," said Tobias. "This place is filthy hot. I'm not sure I could stand it all day." Tobias worked under Ricardo, as he had for a few years now, and was just as keen to find the remnants of the probe. The contents were priceless.

"What do you think?" Ricardo examined the undergrowth and could see no further sign of the probe. He scanned around, but even if there was something there, it was well hidden. The jungle was hot and humid, and he constantly had to keep wiping the sweat that dripped over his eyes.

Tobias pointed up at the canopy. "When it broke up, some of it must have crashed through here. Right above us, actually. See how those branches up there are broken?"

"That doesn't necessarily mean it was our probe," countered Ricardo.

"Maybe. But the island is deserted, right? So, if it wasn't monkeys, then what broke those branches?"

"A storm? Hurricane, perhaps?"

"Not in this area. This far west of the Yasawas, they don't experience tropical storms often. It's the wrong time of year anyway. And don't tell me the tree is old. It's healthy, young. This is the spot all right."

Ricardo shielded his eyes as he looked up. Sunlight filtered through an opening in the tall trees, bursting apart the thick green leaves that dripped with sweat. For the last two hours, he had been trudging slowly through the tall grass and weaving between the trees looking for evidence of where the probe had landed. This was the first real clue they had found. It was a relief to know they were at least on the right trail. The small opening above them gave him a glimpse of blue sky and he suddenly found himself feeling claustrophobic. The trees and bushes swarmed around him, constantly pushing and tugging at his clothes, snaring him. He wanted to be back on the boat, letting Tobias take care of it. Yet he knew he had to keep going. The probe was more important than anything else. He had to go on.

"Okay, let's go and keep an eye out for any more clues as to the probe's location." Ricardo tugged the straps of his backpack, pushing away the thoughts that the island was closing in around him. It was just his imagination. Nobody lived on the island and the nearest people were miles away. There was nothing to be scared of. Yet he was unnerved. He was more at home in front of a computer. He wasn't an explorer. He hated gardening, and he hated the heat. The cool confines of his office cubicle were where he felt at home. He could analyze data from the probe for hours on end and be perfectly happy. Out here, he was exposed, naked, unprepared; he hated it.

"Let's go up there. There's a clearer path," said Tobias. He saw a narrow opening through the jungle. Some of the tree trunks were naturally curving toward the east, perhaps looking for the sun, and there was a path between them. It would be nice to not have to hack their way through the undergrowth for a change. His arms ached and every finger ached from heaving his machete. They each had one and had been forced to use them on several occasions to get through the scrub that blocked their way.

"Excellent. You go on, Tobias. I'll be right behind you. I'll just wait a moment for Jane. If you find anything, radio me and wait. Don't be a hero."

"Got it." Tobias smiled and held up his short-wave radio. "Find the probe. Don't be a hero."

Ricardo watched him go. He was not just a colleague but a friend. They had worked closely over the last two years. What had started out as coffee and donuts over endless data about the mission had progressed into barbecues around each other's homes on summer evenings. Their wives got on well too and Ricardo was happy with his life. He loved his job—apart from when he had to go out in the field to recover lost probes in unexplored jungles on remote islands. That part was not in his job description when he had signed up to working for Space54. It had been a big step leaving NASA, a leap of faith, but the opportunity was just too good to miss. If he had stayed in his position at NASA, then they might have had a crack at Mars in another fifteen to twenty years. Funding and public support dropped every year in equal measure. Going private made sense. Space54 was self-funded and had a definite plan: Mars within five years. They had the finances to back up their ambitious goals and the experts to help them achieve it. Ricardo was just one of many people working on the project. It had been, so far, a complete success. The probe had made it, despite the opinions from the so-called experts in the media and the scientific community who thought they couldn't do it. Ricardo had proved them all wrong. They had made it and got the probe onto the surface of Mars successfully at the first attempt. In truth, there could be no second chances. Several hundred million dollars meant everything had been poured into that one rover. There was no real back-up plan. It was the first time anyone had successfully landed anything on Mars. They managed to get the probe to collect rock samples from where it had landed, and after one orbit, got it to take off again. It had almost been the perfect mission. Only when it was re-entering orbit around Earth had something gone wrong. A simple malfunction with the thrusters had meant it had gone off course, coming down over this forsaken island instead of a planned location in the Atlantic. The probe had begun to disintegrate as it crashed uncontrolled through the Earth's atmosphere. They had been lucky it hadn't crashed into a major city anywhere. The lawsuits would have bankrupted Space54, despite the vast millions backing the company. The problem that they had now was that all that valuable data they had collected was buried somewhere on this island. The local chief had been reluctant to give them access, and it was only a very large donation that had secured the three of them any time at all. They were six hours into what was going to be a grueling journey to find any trace of the probe. Failure was not an option. To have achieved so much only for it all to end like this would be more than frustrating. It was everything to Ricardo. His fledgling marriage could endure any ups and downs, he was sure of that, but his career was on the line now. This was his life.

"Sorry, I'm okay now."

Ricardo watched Jane appear from behind a tree. She looked terrible. Her long blonde hair was tied in a bunch and dark spots of sweat peppered her shirt. Her face was pale, and she wiped her mouth as she approached him.

"You feeling any better?" he asked genuinely. "I know this is difficult, but we found something. We're getting closer, I think."

"Yeah, a little. I don't think I have anything left inside of me to throw up," she said sheepishly. "I'm not good with boats, and this heat…fuck."

"I know." Ricardo could see the journey had taken its toll on her. She knew it was a short trip, and he was impressed she had even volunteered to come along. She was young and pretty, and had no end of admirers back at the company headquarters in Richmond where they worked. She could have taken the easy option and let someone else come along, but she was dogmatic, stubborn, and highly intelligent. The truth was, he was glad to have her with them.

"You okay to carry on? If not, you can head back to the beach and wait for Freddy." Ricardo glanced at his watch. "He'll bring the boat back around in about ten hours. There's no shame in admitting that this is—"

"No, I'm fine." Jane stood upright and looked at Ricardo. She attempted a smile and brushed a fly from her face. "I am *fine*. Show me what you found and let's get this done. I'm not getting back on that boat without getting what we came for."

He could see that she meant it too. He could insist she go back, that she wasn't physically up for the challenge that lay ahead, but it would be pointless. He knew she would just double-back and follow them. There was no way that any of them would leave the island without a piece of Mars in their hands. He would be best to keep her close so he could watch her. She could protest as much as she wanted to, but the truth was she wasn't well. The journey and the dire heat of the jungle was affecting her. He couldn't afford to let it cloud her judgement. If he sent her back to the beach, she might easily get lost. The only way back home was if all three of them stuck together and found the probe together.

"Okay, that way. Tobias went on ahead." Ricardo showed Jane the piece of metal they'd found. "We think it came down close by. Tobias thinks—"

The ground shuddered and the leaves on the trees around them shook. It felt like a tremor and Ricardo looked nervously at Jane. "You felt that, right?"

"Yeah. Weird." Jane looked at a tree close by that was still shaking. The ground had settled down and the flies continued to buzz around her head. "Quake?"

"Possibly, but we're not on any fault line. At least nothing we know of."

"Come on, let's catch up with Tobias. I don't want him finding the probe and claiming all the glory."

Ricardo dismissed the trembling trees. It must have been a shallow quake. It was nothing. He was pleased to see Jane smiling. With an empty stomach, he didn't know how much energy she had in her and he had to make use of her while he could. "Too right. The three of us are in this together. We'll *all* take the glory."

Ricardo followed Jane through the clearing and watched her follow Tobias' trail. They walked for several minutes before reaching a dead end. The trees closed in on them and the thick grass was at least five feet high. There was no sign of Tobias.

"Where is he?" asked Jane. She looked puzzled. "I thought you said he came this way?"

"He did." Ricardo examined the floor, looking for footprints or a clue as to where Tobias had gone.

"What if he wandered off and got hurt, Ricardo? You said we should stay together. You said—"

"I know what I said, Jane," snapped Ricardo. Some of the grass had been flattened and he was sure it had to be from Tobias.

"Tobias?" Jane called out. She looked around but saw nothing. "Tobias, where are you?"

Ricardo felt sick. If something had happened, he was going to have to face Tobias' wife. He was going to have to explain how he had let Tobias go off on his own. This was his responsibility. Yet despite how bad he felt, one thought kept bouncing around his head: now there were only two of them left to find the probe.

"Check me out!"

Jane and Ricardo looked up and saw Tobias sitting in the tree above them. His legs dangled either side of a thick branch and he was grinning and waving at them.

"I feel like a kid again!" he yelled out. "And I can see for freaking *miles*."

"Tobias, what the hell are you doing up there?" Jane anxiously approached the base of the tree. She could see now where he had climbed it. The lower branches were short and stubby, and the large green leaves didn't really get in the way until halfway up. "Get down here."

"You feeling better, Jane?"

She nodded. "Yes, but I'll feel much better when you get down and tell me what's going on. Ricardo told me you found something."

"Yeah, come on Tobias, quit messing about. It's going to take all three of us to hack our way through this jungle." Ricardo looked at the tall grass blocking their way. It was never-ending. He looked up and saw Tobias had his machete tucked into his belt. "Get down here and we'll find the trail again. The probe is close, right?"

Tobias nodded. He pulled apart two huge leaves that were as large as him. "Yeah, it's close. I can see it," he said calmly.

"What? You can *see* it?" asked Jane excitedly.

"Really, Tobias?" Ricardo felt a chill run down his back. The sticky heat, the towering trees, the fear, and nausea all vanished. They had found it. They were going home.

"So, where the fuck is it?" Jane shouted up to Tobias. "Show us."

"Through there." Tobias pointed to the north from where he was perched high in the tree. "There's a ridge just through these trees where the land falls away. There's a huge peak to the side there. Thank God we don't have to climb that. The trees thin out on the other side of it, and I can see the probe lying on the ground, right out in the open. Well, what's left of it anyway. It's pretty smashed up. At the base, I can see a small beach. There's a spit, it's quite small, and it leads over to a smaller island. It's just a rocky outcrop really. If we can get—"

The ground shook again and Ricardo felt Jane grab him. A few leaves fluttered down around them and Ricardo looked up at Tobias. "Okay, maybe you should come down now. You've got it figured out, right? How we can best reach the probe? I don't think it's safe for you to stay up there."

The trembling faded once more and Tobias looked down. "Yeah, I've got it. I can find it. Jesus, what was that? I felt one a few minutes ago too. You don't think that was a quake, do you?" Tobias carefully pulled himself up into a standing position. He gripped the thick trunk and began to move around it, reaching his left foot down for a shorter branch.

"I don't know, Tobias, just get down here." Ricardo felt Jane let go of him and he took out his machete. He approached the nearby grass and took a swing at it. A huge clump fell away under his sharp blade. "We're going to have to do a little more work to get to the probe."

"Be right there," said Jane. "I just want to make sure Tobias is okay. It's always easier going up than down."

"And you know that how?" asked Ricardo as he cleaved apart the grass.

"I have four older brothers, you know." Jane smiled, remembering the farm she grew up on. "You really think I don't know how to climb a tree?"

"Fair call." Ricardo paused to wipe the sweat from his face. "Just make sure that you—"

The ground shook again, this time accompanied by a sound that Ricardo couldn't identify. It sounded like the roar of a lion, only with more base, as if the lion was fifty feet tall. He stopped hacking at the grass and turned to Jane. The ground was still shaking and continued as he looked at her.

"Ricardo?" Jane took her machete out. It wasn't for the grass. "Ricardo, what is that?"

He looked around the jungle, but all he could see was green vegetation. He saw flies and dirt. He saw slivers of sunlight filtering through the branches above and he saw panic on Jane's face. But he didn't see what was causing the ground to shake or the source of the roar.

"Tobias, hurry the fuck up." Jane looked up at Tobias. He was still thirty feet above them, slowly crawling down the tree. Somehow, he seemed to have found the tallest tree on the island. His arms were wrapped around the tree trunk and she saw him glance over his shoulder. His excitement at finding the probe had gone. Now he looked scared, terrified almost. "Tobias?"

"Jane, go back," he shouted. He looked to the east through a gap in the leaves of the tree. "Go, now. Forget the probe."

"What the hell is he talking about?" Ricardo ignored the trembling ground and the dead leaves that shifted beneath his feet. He approached Jane at the base of the tree. He saw a line of ants crawling up the bark, a procession of soldiers heading for home. "Tobias? What do you see?"

"Oh my God."

They didn't hear Tobias whisper. They didn't see what he did. They had no idea what was coming.

"Tobias!" Jane screamed as he let go of the tree. He seemed to push himself away, as if he hadn't slipped but actually wanted to get off the tree. She saw him fall, but there was no scream as he fell. He plummeted to the ground silently, and just as she thought his body was going to crash into the earth next to her, she heard a rustling of leaves. Jane covered her eyes and felt Ricardo grab her.

The ground shook fiercely, sending crashing waves of fear through her. Something wet and warm splashed over the back of her head, and she felt Ricardo's hands push her to the ground. She put her hands out to stop herself falling and landed painfully on the ground. A thick blade of glass sliced open her left palm and she felt Ricardo land beside her. She wiped her eyes and looked at him next to her on the ground. He was staring up at the sky, his face full of shock and awe.

"We should never have come here," he said. Ricardo fumbled for Jane. His fingers found her waist and he clutched at her khaki shirt. "Oh, Jesus. We shouldn't be here."

Jane heard crunching noises from behind her and she turned over to see what Ricardo was looking at. Tobias was back in the tree, only his face was flat and lifeless, and his arms no longer waving but hanging limply by his side. Blood dripped copiously from his body that had been severed at the waist. His intestines dribbled from his exposed guts, and Jane knew what had splattered the back of her head. She didn't need to look to know. Looking at him, she felt oddly calm. He was dead, plain and simple. There was no coming back from it. What troubled her more was what had killed him. A giant monster, as tall as the trees, had him held tightly in two front claws. Its head and arms poked through the foliage, but the bulk of what was undoubtedly a massive body was hidden by the thick copse of trees. The thing was unrecognizable. It was no creature that she had ever seen or dreamt of. In between the lush green leaves she spied its eyes, two bright blue orbs that seemed to stare at her and Ricardo. Slowly, she saw the thing lift Tobias' body up through the branches of the tree and into its mouth. It snapped off an arm and began to chew on the bone and meat.

Tobias had seen it. She remembered how he had pushed himself away from the tree he had climbed. Somehow, he had seen it coming and tried to escape it. The monster must have plucked him right from the air as he fell. That meant it had quick reflexes. No matter how huge this thing was, she was going to have to outsmart it. All her pain and nausea from the journey here had gone. She was in survival mode now. It was odd. She had never been in a dangerous situation before. She'd never been in a fight, even at school, and had backed away from difficult situations at all times. Her brothers had teased her throughout childhood, but they also protected her. Now she was going to have to learn how to fight for herself.

With the monster crunching Tobias' bones, it seemed to be distracted. Whilst it was apparently watching them from the hidden sanctuary of the trees, it wasn't moving and it wasn't coming for them. Jane thought logically. They had a chance to get out of this. She wanted to go home. She wanted to find the probe, but more than that she wanted to live. Jane looked around her. There was no path, no escape. She was surrounded by trees. She kept her body still and ignored the throbbing pain in her hand, using only her eyes to scan around her. The grass. The tall grass would give them some cover from the creature. If they could get to it before the thing, they might have a chance. They could hide, perhaps find an uprooted tree and hide in its roots. Perhaps they could squeeze in between the rocks on the far side of the ridge where it couldn't reach them. Jane knew she had to try. As the monster lifted Tobias up to its mouth again and snapped off his other arm, she knew they didn't have much time. Tobias wasn't going to keep it busy much longer. She doubted his body was much of a meal. They had to go now.

Jane slowly turned her head to Ricardo. "Look at me, Ricardo," she whispered. "We need to run to the tall grass."

Ricardo turned his face to hers. He looked ruined. He looked more scared than she had seen anyone before in her life. He shook his head from side to side.

"No. Play dead. It'll leave soon."

Jane glanced at the creature. Its head was poking through the highest branches of the trees and its blue eyes were firmly fixed on them. "*No*. It knows we're here. It's watching us. We have to go. We stay here and we die."

Ricardo swallowed as flies swarmed around his feet. They were drenched with blood. Tobias' blood. He shook his head again. "No, I'm staying here. It doesn't want us. It got... it got Tobias. Let's wait."

Jane felt despondent. She couldn't do it without Ricardo. She couldn't leave him and yet she didn't want to wait. She knew that would mean a horrible death. She had to make him understand that running was their best option, their *only* option. Carefully, she felt around her on the flat ground. Her machete was close, and she gently wrapped her fingers around the shaft. Her left hand ached and was slippery with blood so she kept her eyes locked on the monster as she maneuvered the machete to her right hand. The monster continued to mangle Tobias body, ignoring her. As she watched it chew on his dead body, she was reminded of her cat Ginger. On the lucky occasions that he caught a mouse or a bird, he would chew on it just like that. Eating it was only part of it. Ginger did it because he could, as if he wanted to prove he was king of the jungle. This thing was the same. It was playing a game with then, teasing them into doing something, or nothing. It didn't care. It oozed superiority. Whatever it was, it was king of the jungle here. They were no more than a bird to be broken, killed and eaten.

"Ricardo, in ten seconds, I am getting up and running for that tall grass." Jane pulled her knees up and prepared to jump up. Once she was on her feet, she knew she had precious little time to make the line of grass. There was only a few feet between her and it, and she could make it in only a couple of seconds. But the monster was huge, and no matter how large and heavy it was, it was probably quick on its feet. She didn't know how much time she had, but she had to take the chance she had. She would have a head start on it, and those extra few seconds might mean all the difference between living or dying. "You can come with me or you can wait here to die. What are you going to do?"

She meant every word. Her fear had given her an adrenalin rush. She wanted to see her brothers again, to go back to the farm she grew up on. She was going to run for her life, with or without him.

"What is it?" whispered Ricardo.

"What are you going to do?" asked Jane again. She nudged his body with the machete and glared at him. "Well?"

Ricardo slowly nodded. She saw that he still had his machete in his hand. Whether he accepted their situation or not, she knew he was ready to run. The sound of Tobias being eaten was too much. She pointed to the tall grass, just a few feet away and then glanced at the monster. Its blue eyes still seemed to be watching her, but she had no choice. She couldn't sit back and wait. She had to do something. She looked at Ricardo.

"We go together. Ready?"

Ricardo nodded and she saw tears fall from his eyes. They might have been for Tobias or for themselves, but she thought they were probably for his family. He had a wife and a child. It was good that he was thinking of them. They would give him a reason to run faster than he ever had before. She had no husband or children, but she sure as hell wasn't about to give up.

"Three," she whispered.

She didn't feel like crying. She felt like fighting. This island had quickly turned into a nightmare. The clear blue sky and white sandy beach they had arrived on was barely a memory. Jane prepared to run.

"Two," she said as she looked at Ricardo.

She remembered the happiness on Tobias' face when he told them he had found the probe. How quickly things could change. One minute he was part of a team bringing the most important scientific discovery to mankind, the next he was dead, his corpse in the mouth of a terrifying monster. His blood was splattered all over her, over Ricardo, and the jungle floor. Jane gripped her machete. That monster wasn't going to take her. She eyed the tall line of grass. She was going to run. She was going to get out of this. She steeled herself and stared at Ricardo.

"One."

Jane jumped up and pulled Ricardo to his feet. "Go!"

Jane began to run. Her feet smacked loudly across the jungle floor flattening the grass and ants, and she felt the ground shaking. There was a deafening roar behind her and the sound of branches snapping. Sweat stung her eyes as she ran for the grass, her heart pounding so fast she thought she might just die of a heart attack.

Ricardo was next to her and she saw a shadow fall over him. From the corner of her eye, she saw the monster. She felt its warm breath behind her and tried to run faster. Her legs were pumping as hard as she could. The tall grass was only three feet away when she saw Ricardo lifted into the air. He screamed and she felt more blood shower down over her. Jane frantically ran for the grass, tears surprising her as they flowed from her eyes. There was a scream, a high-pitched wail that she realized was coming from herself as she charged into the tall grass. The shadow that had encompassed Ricardo fell over her and she pushed apart the first thick blades of grass. As she thrust herself into the thicket, she remembered Ginger and how he had enjoyed chewing on the dead bird's mangled body. Even as the bird twitched, the cat had begun to chew on the delicate meat. Jane cried out and swung her machete around her, hoping that her own death would be quicker and less painful.

CHAPTER 2

The room was stifling. The air-conditioning unit had broken down, again, and Phoenix could feel the sweat rolling down her back. She had spent time in the Middle East—and way too much in the shithole they called Tikrit for her own liking—trekked through the Syrian Desert, trained in the jungles of Borneo, and even spent a little downtime in the Northern Territory of Australia. Yet nothing seemed to compare to the heat of the briefing room aboard the ship currently churning its way through the Pacific Ocean. The humidity, almost ninety-five percent, was so thick that she felt like she couldn't breathe. She untucked her shirt from her khakis. To hell with appearances. It was what she said to them that mattered, not what she looked like. Karl, Alex, Justin, and Darius already knew her and she knew them. They had served together for a few years now, with Alex, the youngest member of the team. They knew she would be focused on the mission and unconcerned with what she looked like. She never had. Prom dresses and curlers held little appeal to her. Ever since she was fifteen, she had found herself drawn to the military. She had cut her hair short, much to her mother's disappointment, taken to wearing plain slacks and T-shirts and hefty boots, and watching old black and white war films on cable. Her parents tried to tell her she was beautiful and that she shouldn't cover it up, that she should go out with boys, to the football, to the mall; do all the other things her friends did. But Phoenix refused to buckle. Her two older sisters followed the party line. Virginia had predictably married an accountant and settled down to have four kids as soon as she could. Tacoma disappeared off to college, found a nice boy-next-door type, all strawberry-blond hair and strong shoulders, and rented a loft in New York where they could plan their Sunday mornings around brunch and runs through Central Park. Phoenix had been out with a few boys but not many had gone beyond the first date. She was too closed, too controlling, too damn masculine. That's what she had been told anyway. The military? That was a career for men, not girls from Oklahoma trying to prove a point.

She pinned the map to the white board behind her, securing each corner with a soggy blob of blue-tac. The corners of the map were curling up, wilting in the heat, and she felt like doing the same. The window behind her was open, but there was no breeze coming in, just the sweet smell of aviation fuel. It was a reminder of the exhausting journey they had taken. The memory of sitting on the plane reminded her that this journey wasn't over yet, not by a long shot. Had they had time to plan it, they would've taken a flight direct to Pago Pago. A nice cruisy eight-hour flight to American Samoa sounded much better than the torturous eighteen-hour journey she had just finished.

From Guam, they had flown to Port Moresby, Papua New Guinea. A hot four-hour wait had ensued before they'd connected onto a flight through to the private airstrip outside of Townsville, Australia. The heat had increased as they had spent another two hours there waiting for the military helicopter that took them to the USS Ronald Reagan, currently on maneuvers in the South Pacific, its precise location undisclosed.

"Damn flies," said Phoenix as she batted another one away.

The ship rolled slightly, but the weather was good; the sea was quite calm, which was more than could be said for her stomach. Phoenix hadn't eaten much in the last few hours. Now she was about to deliver her briefing on the mission ahead, after only learning of it herself since landing on the Reagan forty-five minutes ago. In one hour, they would all be on a Sikorsky. Such was life in the military. Part of her wished she could be more like her sisters, to just settle down and give this up. But a part of her enjoyed it. The travelling and suddenness of it all, the secrecy and operations that would come up unexpectedly was all a part of it. She was still young and had plenty of time to settle down when she was older.

Her body had no idea what time zone it was supposed to be in anymore. Her mind was sharp, and she had no problem with the secrecy of what was happening. It was part of the deal. She had trust in the system and her immediate superiors. The toll on her body from so much travelling though often left her feeling nauseous, so she skipped meals, snacking on power bars now and again. That only made her more nauseous, and until the mission was over, she had a feeling she was just going to have to agree to disagree with her stomach.

She felt a fly crawling on the nape of her neck, its black legs wading through the sweat like a pig digging for truffles. Slapping her hand on her neck, she knew she had missed it, and the fly disappeared. She looked at the map and tried to forget how much her body craved a decent meal and sleep. This was up to her now. The operation and the lives of her unit were reliant on her figuring out just how badly things could go. There was a dullness behind her eyes, and she knew a headache was threatening to burst like a thundercloud inside her head. It would have to wait. She had no time for anything now but to get ready for what lay ahead. The problem was she didn't really know what that was.

The door swung open and four soldiers entered the room, bringing a wave of hot air with them. In turn, they acknowledged her and sat down on flimsy plastic chairs that had been placed to face the front. Phoenix watched them find a seat and then chatter amongst themselves. They had a lot of nervous energy to expel and were eager to get on with it, whatever "it" was.

"Walker, you make sure everyone got a good feed?"

"Yes, ma'am, the chow was pretty damn good."

"Then take a load off and listen up. At ease, everybody. We're all friends here."

Karl Walker, second-in-command, was a good man and a good soldier. Phoenix had to remember that physically he was more than just a stereotype, capable of almost anything. He was a walking, talking cliché in combat boots. Every shirt he wore seemed too small to hide his bulging muscles and recently he had taken to sporting a moustache, as if he needed any more proof that he was full of testosterone. Despite his natural physical authority, he seemed to have a problem serving under her. Phoenix still hadn't worked out if it was because she was a woman or if he simply didn't like her. Still, he knew how to play the game. For all his barbed comments about her leadership, he was biding his time, performing whatever tasks were asked of him to the letter. He would follow her to his death if it meant he got a shot at taking command one day.

"Right, we'll get started then." Phoenix leant back against the metal desk and looked at her crew. Only four soldiers. The next twenty-four hours were supposed to be simple. No danger, just a quick rescue operation. Yet she was worried they might be underestimating the situation. She had tried to reason with her superiors that they should send a full unit, yet it was impossible they had told her. The operation was not exactly above board. The less people involved the better for everyone, she was told. So here she was, facing four of her best men with a million questions that she wasn't sure she would be able to answer.

"I want you all suited and booted in thirty minutes. We're scheduled to depart at 0530 and we'll be airborne for approximately twenty-eight minutes. Our ride is that sweet little number outside on deck, the DCX4539. She'll be a little cramped with the six of us, but she'll do just right. We will be landing on a small atoll, just east of the main island." Phoenix pointed to the map she had pinned up. There was a vast expanse of blue and a small dot in the center that represented the island. "The island is uninhabited, and we do not expect to encounter any hostile forces. We will land at sunrise and leave at dusk. We have a period of nine hours, maximum, to find and retrieve our targets. This is a rescue operation. The terrain could be hostile which is why they need us. We are going fishing for three US citizens who have got themselves into a little trouble it would appear. We are the cavalry."

"You said six of us." Karl looked around the room. "Maybe math isn't your best point, Phoenix, but there's only five of us."

"I realize that we're one short, but I'm—"

Right on cue, the door opened and a man dressed in light blue cotton trousers stepped in. He had an open-necked shirt and sunglasses hanging around his neck on a black cord. He pushed a pair of wire-rimmed glasses up his nose and took a seat quietly at the back of the room.

"Let me introduce you to Max," said Phoenix. "He'll be joining us on this fishing trip. I'm sure like all of us that he's hoping to catch his people alive and well." She pointed to Max who was sat at the back of the room and he stood up to introduce himself. "Max has worked at Space54 for over five years. He is well aware of our operation and briefed on what is expected of him. He will help us to find these people. I expect you all to cooperate fully."

"Space54? What the fuck is that?" asked Karl.

"Nerds," said Darius to his right. "I think they're some kind of private operator trying to send man to Mars or something."

"We prefer the term scientist, but nerd just about covers it, I suppose. And yes, you are quite correct, we are trying to send man to Mars." Max cleared his throat and pushed his glasses up his sweaty nose. "I'm Max Hudson. I've worked at Space54 for over seven years actually. Before that, I was at NASA. I can tell you that I am just hoping I can help you find our people. They are very important to us, and I'll do what I can to get them home. All three of them are sorely missed. You can imagine how distraught their families are."

"Max is a doctor, and I'm glad we have him with us," said Phoenix, indicating that he should sit down. She wasn't glad about having him at all, but Space54 had insisted they have one of their own go to the island and there was no getting around it. Orders were orders. Phoenix returned to face her unit as Max sat down. "The fact that we've been unable to establish the whereabouts of these three employees or their status means we have to assume one or more of them is injured, possibly seriously. I know we have basic medical training, but Space54 wanted one of their own on this. He can help us identify the... scientists." Phoenix caught herself from saying victims. She had to keep the vibe positive. Nobody wanted to waste their time going looking for three dead bodies. "I am assured that we have your full co-operation, Max."

He nodded quietly and Phoenix hoped he was on the level. She didn't like taking strangers, but she was under orders. Apparently, Max had served in the army in his youth before joining NASA and then more recently Space54. She was assured he would not interfere. They just wanted to get their people home, preferably alive, but in body bags if they had to. He looked harmless, and she could tell he was keen to get going. They had met briefly before the meeting and he had approached her with a warm handshake. He was dressed completely inappropriately for what they were doing. When the briefing was over, she would make sure Karl got him in a more suitable attire. They had to have a spare uniform around somewhere. The glasses perched atop his thin nose did nothing to dispel the thought that he was out of his depth. A scientist and a doctor had no place on a rescue operation like this. Still, as long as he did what she said, she would let him get on with helping find the three missing people.

"Anyone else we got to babysit?" asked Karl.

Phoenix felt him glaring at her. He could piss his pants all he liked, but they both knew he would do what he had to. There was no discussion.

"The team is comprised of me and you, of course, Karl. Lucky for us, huh?"

"Yeah, we're regular buddies." Karl smirked and looked around the room. "She doesn't like to go anywhere without me. Ain't that right, Justin?"

"Bet your last dollar on it."

Phoenix sighed. "Well, for Max's sake, we should do introductions. We don't have much time, so I'll keep it brief. I see no reason to stand on ceremony on this operation. First names will be fine. Max, this is Karl, my second-in-command. Do what he says and you'll be just fine." Tiresome though he was, Phoenix had to admit she could trust him when they had business to do. He was a tough soldier, weather-worn and rough around the edges, but a hard worker. He was on the level and was thinking the same as her; it was a bad idea to take Max along. She had her orders to follow, and so did Karl, so they would both just have to suck it up. Sometimes, she admired Karl and the way he had no filter. He had the freedom of sharing his thoughts openly not being in charge, but all that would change once he was in control of his own unit and answerable to superior powers.

Karl nodded as Phoenix pointed out the others in the room. "Darius Jackson, medic and comms. All round good guy, right, Darius?"

"Oh, I can be bad if you want me to," he said, grinning.

Phoenix liked Darius. He was a joker, but in the field, he was utterly reliable. He didn't have a problem with following a woman. It might be because he was black. Perhaps he had more of an understanding of being up against it. His jokes were a way of making light of the situation and were never too harsh, unlike Karl's. He used humor as a form of attack.

"Max, the young man you're sat behind is Justin Cartwright."

Justin saluted Phoenix and turned to shake Max's hand, smiling. "I know what you're thinking," he said as he rifled his hand through a shock of red hair. "I'm too young and pretty to be a soldier. Well, I can shoot the hairs off a nun's ass from a hundred yards."

More laughter rippled throughout the room.

"Yeah, he's a real hotshot," said Karl.

"You know it, brother."

Phoenix smiled weakly. Let them get it out of their system. Once they were on the island, the jokes would stop. She knew she could rely on them once she got them out of the locker room and into battle.

"Thanks, Justin, you can sit your ass down now." Phoenix saw Max smirk. Did the old man really know what he had let himself in for? "Alex Paige, stand up and wave to the crowd."

The soldier sat behind Karl got up and nodded to Max. "Pleased to meet you, sir. We'll get your guys back. This here is the best team I've ever worked with."

Phoenix watched Alex sit down. He was young too, like Justin, but they were completely different. He didn't joke around like the others. His head was always shaved perfectly and his boots spotless. He took the job seriously, and if he kept it up, she could see him working his way up through the ranks. He was in it for a long career. Justin would always be a soldier and a good one too, but he had no ambitions of climbing the ladder.

"So, six of us, that's it?" asked Karl.

"Seven actually."

Karl sighed and raised his eyebrows. "Who now? President Trump wants to come along? Britney Spears? You've got to be kidding me. We don't take tourists with us, Phoenix, you know that. You got Peter fucking Pan waiting in the helicopter for us?"

Phoenix smiled and turned around to point at the map. "We're going to drop in here." She pointed to a small dot on a vast blue map. Most of it was ocean. "It's a small atoll about five kilometers from the actual island. It's as close as we can get. The island itself is covered in thick jungle. The beaches are too small to get in, so the only access is by sea. We'll be meeting a local guide, Freddy, who will take us over to the island. He can show us where he left the three targets and give us an overview of what the island is like. It's uncharted and nobody quite knows what it'll be like. We need him. I understand he has been briefed to give us all the help we require."

"Phoenix, why don't we just sail the *Reagan* right up its ass?" asked Darius. "Why can't we just drop right onto the island and get this over with?"

"I'm afraid there is some difficulty with access," said Max. "Do you mind?"

Phoenix let Max take the floor. The old man stood and approached her cautiously, much as if he were approaching a lion. *He had been out of the game for a long time*, she thought. Karl was right. They were going to have to babysit him the whole time.

"You see, the island in question is off limits." Max stood next to Phoenix and addressed the room. "It is uninhabited and part of the Yasawa Islands, ruled by the local chief. He does not allow visitors. Many of the islands in this area of the South Pacific are completely untouched by man. He granted Space54 access two days ago to retrieve a lost probe, and it took a lot of pressure to get him to allow us that one window. Unfortunately, that window has closed, and—"

"And that's where we come in, right?" Karl looked at Phoenix. "This is bullshit," he muttered.

"We have one day. We will go in at dawn, find the three missing people, and get out. Nobody will know we were there. Officially, we will be on our own. The chief won't allow anyone to visit the island."

"You mean this Space54 company won't dig their hands into their pockets and pay him enough to get back there," said Karl.

"Trust me, we tried," said Max. He looked downcast. "Those poor people don't deserve to be left out there. What if they're not dead? What if they had an accident or got lost? I knew Ricardo and Tobias quite well. They are astrophysicists and very astute men. I've been seeing them for their annual physical the last few years. Jane is relatively new to the organization but from what I know a wonderful woman. Ricardo has two sons. Jane is so young that if anything happened to her—"

He tailed off. Phoenix could see he was upset. She guessed she would be too if she lost someone close to her. That was probably why she didn't let anyone get too close. A career in the military helped with that. There were plenty of testosterone-filled soldiers around when she needed a quick pick-me-up, but she would rather live her life on her own. Her sisters and parents were all she'd ever needed.

"Space54. What kind of funky name is that for a multi-billion-dollar company?" asked Darius. "Sounds like a kid's cartoon if you ask me."

"And what about this probe shit?" Alex looked apologetic when he spoke. "Sorry, I just mean this sounds like it should be a private operation. Some rich-ass company lost a spaceship and three of their own employees. Why are we involved?"

"Good question, Alex," said Karl, staring at Phoenix. "Why *are* we involved?"

"It seems that the island might be a little more dangerous than we anticipated," countered Max. "Something has happened, and it is beyond our resources to perform a rescue operation. We are scientists, not soldiers. We need your help."

"So, get Special Forces. Ring Fort Bragg and give them your sob story," said Karl.

"Sounds odd to me," said Justin. "Space54 has more money than NASA."

"And if this is such a delicate operation, why only send the five of us?" asked Darius. "Half the squad is still back in Guam. Why us?"

"Look, this is supposed to be a quick in and out." Phoenix was feeling exasperated. There were too many questions. She didn't like it either, but they had a job to do. "It's a simple extraction. We will locate the two men and one woman that Space54 lost and bring them back. The local chief will not allow Space54 access to the island. Period. We are going in under the radar, both literally and metaphorically. Nobody outside this room and a couple of people higher up the chain knows about this. Understand?"

"I understand that if this goes wrong, we are completely fucked, and Space54 walks away scot-free," said Karl. "I hope you know what you're getting us into, Phoenix."

"I spoke directly to General Greene of the USARPAC earlier. Our orders are clear, Walker." The tone in Phoenix's voice was clear. Karl understood when to push it and when to shut it.

"What about the skipper of the boat, this Freddy guy?" asked Darius nervously. "How come he's helping us?"

"He was the one who called it in." Max looked at Phoenix for approval to speak and she nodded. He wiped a bead of sweat running down his cheek and went on. "Freddy is just a local guide. When the team from Space54 didn't return, he went to the island himself. He told our guys that he looked around but couldn't find any trace of our people. The chief doesn't know that he's helping us. Freddy just feels responsible for what happened. He wants to help. He'll be an asset to us, not a liability. Truly."

"Yeah, and I bet you found a way to make sure he stays quiet, right?" Karl rubbed his thumb and fingers together, imagining them full of cash.

Max ignored Karl. "Freddy also said that he heard strange noises coming from the island."

"Noises?"

"Don't ask. It was just local superstition. The local tribe believes that the island is a resting place for the spirits of their ancestors. That's why we must tread carefully. Nobody is allowed on the island, and Space54 went to a lot of trouble getting our people on there. The noises and rumors are just that, stories designed to scare children at night and keep people away."

"And this probe of yours that crashed on the island?" Phoenix turned to Max. "What about that? Any dangerous substances or anything we need to know?"

Max shook his head and looked at the door. He lowered his voice as he answered and Phoenix wondered if he was about to burst into tears. "Ricardo, Tobias, and Jane were going to retrieve our data. There's nothing dangerous about the probe. Much of it broke up on re-entry. There are some samples that it collected, but our focus is our people."

"Samples? Like from *Mars*?"

Max glanced at Phoenix. "Yes. Just some small rocks from the surface, I believe. I was not involved in that side of things, so I couldn't really speculate."

"Maybe those noises the local guy heard weren't his dead ancestors but aliens," suggested Darius. "The start of a Klingon invasion. Maybe a Martian hitched a ride back to planet Earth on that spacecraft."

"Come on, Darius, Klingons don't exist," said Karl.

"Yeah, it was more likely Stormtroopers," said Alex. "Getting their ray-guns ready."

"Idiot." Justin punched Alex on the shoulder. "Ray-guns are Star Trek, not Star Wars."

"Look, ladies, I deal with facts. And the facts are this." Phoenix stood in front of her depleted unit and folded her arms. She looked studiously at each member of her team. None of them were scared. None of them thought this mission was worth a damn. She could see it in their eyes. This was a joke to them. But if they didn't take it seriously, they were liable to come unstuck. She had to make then focus, not dream of little green men. "We are entering the unknown here. Fact one: the rover crashed somewhere on that island and the terrain may be hostile. It is a hot, tropical jungle that will kick your ass if you're not focused. Fact two: The only three people who have ever stepped foot on that place didn't come back. So we have to deal with whatever we might find. Nobody has explored the island. The terrain is going to be difficult. It's going to beyond hot. Something like fifty degrees. At night, it'll freeze, which is why we want to be out of there before the sun sets. There is no Wi-Fi or cell reception. There is no Seven

Eleven. There is no Starbucks or Holiday Inn, so sure, get your laughing and your jokes done now, but the second we leave this room, the laughing stops. Three people may have already lost their lives, and I'm not going in unprepared or treating this like some kind of school trip. You *will* follow my orders and come home alive. Anyone who gets themselves dead has got *me* answer to. Got that?"

"Yes, Staff Sergeant," snapped her team almost in unison.

Phoenix looked at Karl. He wanted her job, no doubt about it, but until he was prepared to knuckle down and forget screwing around with his buddies, he was a long way short of taking it from her. Tact and diplomacy weren't exactly her strongest traits, but she knew how to follow orders, how to cope in difficult situations, and how to know when she should keep her mouth shut. Karl would always be her junior until he learnt that.

"Who exactly are these three people we're looking for?" asked Karl folding his arms.

Phoenix turned to the board behind her, picked up three headshots, and stuck them up. She pointed out each one as she put their photograph up on display. "All science geeks employed by Space54. Tobias Cleaver, Jane Lenovar, and the team leader, Ricardo Mendez. They were supposed to find their lost probe, get whatever data they could from it, and be back home right now watching reruns of Dexter."

"Nerds," muttered Darius. "Three lost nerds. That's all we need."

"Boy, are they gonna be glad to see us," said Justin.

"With your IQ, Justin, I can just imagine the conversation now. Them talking about interplanetary travel, you talking about hot dogs." Darius chuckled. "Dazzling."

Phoenix ignored them.

"Weapons?" asked Karl seriously.

"We'll be going in light," said Phoenix. "This is a search-and-rescue operation, not a seek-and-destroy. There's no reason to believe we'll encounter anything more aggressive than sunburn and sandflies. We won't be there long enough to find out if there's anything more. We will need a couple of machetes though. Walker, make sure you get them. The island has a lot of vegetation we need to get through. We don't want to be held up just because there's no sidewalk. It's going to be hard work so don't forget them."

Phoenix gave them little else about the mission. There wasn't much else she could tell them. General Greene had been sketchy on details with her. It was clearly a covert operation, and the less she knew, the better. She had a feeling that the CEO of Space54 had pulled some strings to get General Greene involved. People like that had friends in high places. The general had given nothing away and told it to her straight: get the Space54 employees and get out. That about summed up her job. She had no problem following orders, no matter how unusual or secretive they were, but even she had to admit this was highly irregular. It felt like they weren't being given the whole picture, but the Space54 doctor, Max, seemed to be just as clueless on the situation. For now, all she could do was go along with it and get the men fully prepared. She ordered them all to get their gear ready and for Karl to ensure that Max was suitably prepared. As they began to leave, she heard them talking amongst themselves and turned her back to them. She hoped she had made them realize that no matter how easy the task seemed, they still had to take it, and her, seriously. She had seen too many good people take their eye off the ball and end up fucked up to accept anything less.

"She good?"

Phoenix heard the doctor mutter it under his breath. Out of her peripheral vision, she noticed he was walking out with Karl.

"Yeah, she's good."

She was almost surprised by the secret seal of approval from him. They had served together in Iraq but never made much of a friendship out of it. Rarely did she hear him say anything positive about her command.

"Fifi's all bark and no bite. Don't worry, Doc, we'll find your men. Just stick with me."

The approval he had just given her was bullshit. She knew Karl had said what he'd said to Max just loud enough for her to hear. He wanted her to know that he was undermining her already. It was a challenge she had faced numerous times before, simply for being a woman. It didn't matter that she had two tours in Iraq under her belt or ten years' service. Karl took any opportunity he could to stick the knife in and give it a little twist. In a moment of weakness last year, when she thought they were bonding instead of butting heads, and she had admittedly drunk one too many Singapore Slings, she had confessed her childhood nickname was Fifi. Now, when he was trying to wind her up, he brought it out. Rising to the bait would be too easy.

She heard the footsteps fade and the door close. Turning around to an empty room, she sighed and looked at the clock. Karl could throw his toys, but it didn't matter. He would follow her just as he did every time they were sent somewhere hot and horrible. They had a job to do. There were three American citizens out there, possibly hurt, who were relying on them to get home. No, not relying on them, on *her*. She was in charge, and no matter how good a unit she had, the responsibility was on her to get everyone back. It was going to be a long day.

Phoenix slapped the back of her neck and looked at her palm.

"Got you," she said victoriously.

The dead fly left a tiny trace of blood on her skin, and she smiled with satisfaction as she wiped the dead bug on her thigh. The sweat rolled down her neck and she strode out of the room onto the deck of the ship. The scorching sun was hidden behind her and the sky was a pure blue, with not a hint of cloud anywhere. The jungle they were heading to would be at least ten degrees hotter.

It was going to be a very long day indeed.

CHAPTER 3

The helicopter drop was easy. The atoll was just a thin stretch of sand surrounded by coral and miles of flat ocean. A couple of palm trees at one end were the only vegetation on the island. The sun was just a blur of orange on the horizon and the early morning air was cool. The Sikorsky took off when they were all safely on the ground, sending sand flying around them. When it was finally gone, the stillness and silence descended over them like a warm blanket.

"Hoorah," said Justin as he dropped his pack onto the sand and removed his cap. "And I'm getting paid for this?"

"Sure is sweet." Alex looked around at the vast expanse of blue surrounding them. "What do you say, Squad Leader, shall we just camp here for the day?"

"Yeah, come on, it's not every day you get paid to go to paradise." Justin yawned. "I could knock up a hammock between those two trees. You guys catch up with me later when we have our targets in the bag."

"No deal," said Karl. "And pick your shit up, Private. Our ride's here."

A small boat that had been waiting fifty feet from shore was chugging slowly toward them. Phoenix thought that it looked like it would barely fit them all, and it was hardly seaworthy. There was no shelter and just a small outboard motor fixed to the rear. She saw a dark-skinned man steer the boat up close to the island and then cut the engine. The boat was no more than twenty feet long, and the man pulled up what looked like a ladder from the deck. He attached one end by two hooks to the aft and then dropped the other end in the ocean. It was about ten feet from the sand, although the water was shallow.

"Looks like we're going to get our feet wet." Karl ordered the men to get on board. "This guy's on the level, right?"

Phoenix nodded. "He's been checked out. He'll get us to the island."

"He was the last man to see them alive," said Max as he began rolling up his pants around his ankles. "The island is about thirty minutes from here. I want to talk to him and find out what he knows. He might be able to—"

"I've got it covered, Doc," said Karl. "I'll talk to him with the staff sergeant. You sit in the back of the boat and try not to get in our way."

"Thanks." Phoenix nodded to Max that he should go. She watched him awkwardly walk up the ladder onto the boat where Justin and Darius helped him climb in.

"Keep an eye on him, Karl. I don't think he'll cause us any trouble, but we don't want any tourists getting in our way. We've already got three civilians to find, I don't want to make that four."

"Not a problem."

Karl clambered up the ladder skillfully, making light work of it, and Phoenix was the last aboard. As she looked around the small boat, she was reminded of the film Titanic. Her unit was on the deck looking like refugees from a sinking ship. The area of the Pacific Ocean they were in was desolate, and there was no help coming if they fucked up. She felt alone and worried that her men were too vulnerable. Of quite what she wasn't sure, but she wanted to be cautious and find out as much about the island as she could. As Karl gave her a hand into the boat, she helped him pull up the ladder and slide it down out of the way. It was time to talk to their guide, Freddy, and find out what the hell they were getting themselves into.

"Thank you." Karl took a seat on the lip of the boat next to the wheel and Phoenix sat opposite him. The driver was in between them, and he started the engine before pulling away from the atoll.

"Freddy, right?" Phoenix held out her hand and the man took it, shaking her hand with a strength she found surprising. He had an athletic physique and wore a thin cotton shirt that flapped open as they made their way to the island. He smiled as he shook her hand. There was a genuine warmth behind his sparkling blue eyes, and for a moment, Phoenix wondered what he looked like with his shirt off. Karl and her unit were all bulging muscles and XXXL shirts. Freddy was toned, slim, and handsome; even though it was completely inappropriate, she couldn't help but imagine what they could get up to if she was stranded on a tropical island with him.

"Freddy. You must be Staff Sergeant Lethbridge."

"Call me Phoenix." She shoved the impure thoughts to the back of her mind and instantly was back in the zone. *The mission*, she thought, *focus on the mission and not his biceps*. "It's beautiful out here. You think we're in for a blue sky kind of day?"

She wanted him to open up to her, provide them with as much information as possible about the island and potential whereabouts of the three missing people. She felt stupid talking about the weather, but it was a simple way to start a conversation. She knew next to nothing about this man and it seemed like as good a place to start as any.

"Every day is a blue sky day out here," said Freddy, grinning. He looked young, perhaps in his mid-twenties. *Too young for me*, thought Phoenix. Karl was closest in age to her, but he made it clear every day that he wasn't interested in her.

"Try telling that to Ricardo, Tobias, and Jane," said Karl. "I'm thinking they would rather not see another of your blue sky days. Assuming they still have the capability to think."

Freddy instantly lost his gracious smile. "Of course. I feel so desperately sorry for them. I want to help you find your friends."

Too blunt, thought Phoenix. He needed softening up. "Your English is good, Freddy. Where'd you go to school?"

"Suva. I was schooled on my home island of course like everyone else, but I went to college in Suva so I could learn engineering. Boats are more than just a means of getting around out here; they're a way of life. We depend on them. I wanted to make sure I knew everything I could about the mechanics, the engines, everything."

"Smart choice."

"So how come you're out here ferrying tourists around and not earning big bucks on the main island?" asked Karl bluntly.

Phoenix glared at him, but Freddy didn't seem to mind the question.

"I had job offers in Suva and the boatyards, but that's not what I want from life. My people are a poor people, financially. The Yasawa Islands do not have many opportunities to grow and make money except for tourism. I want to make sure that continues and grows. I run a company that needs all my expertise to keep going. I employ fifteen people and am very proud of my home. I want to show the Yasawas off to as many people as I can. This is a beautiful area, so why would I want to leave?"

"Beautiful or dangerous? What about this island you're taking us to?" asked Karl. "Three people may have died in your so-called paradise."

"It is not my *island* that is dangerous," said Freddy looking at Karl's gun. He looked at Phoenix and noticed that she was carrying too. "There is always danger with beauty."

Phoenix felt Freddy's eyes bore into hers. There was that thought again, of a tropical island paradise, of Freddy taking off his shirt as he slowly undressed her, the warm sun on her body. She guiltily glanced at Karl, but he didn't seem to notice anything odd. Phoenix had to remind herself she was in charge here, of not just her own unit but finding three stranded civilians. "Go on, Freddy," she said in as an assertive tone as she could manage as she wilted under Freddy's eyes and the rising sun.

"It is nature." Freddy's eyes drifted back to the ocean and he continued. "A pufferfish looks beautiful, but if you eat it, you'll almost certainly be dead in twenty minutes. The ocean looks beautiful, yet treat it with contempt, and she'll kill you. I have a boat with six strangers on carrying guns. And yet you think my island is dangerous?"

"My squad leader didn't mean any offence," said Phoenix quickly. "Karl's just worried about our people. We all are. They're not used to it out here. Like you said, the ocean can be deadly if you don't know what you're doing. That's why we're so grateful you could help us, Freddy. We sure appreciate any help you can give us. Rest assured that we do not want to cause any trouble for you or your people. The sooner we find our people, the sooner we will leave." Part of her didn't want to leave. Part of her wanted to go back to the atoll and let Justin put up that hammock. "Please, Freddy, we need your help. *I* need your help."

Freddy clammed up and she saw him thinking it over. Karl had pushed him too far. She hoped it wouldn't be too much.

"We're in this together, Freddy," she said. "Discretion is the name of the game. We're not looking to get you into trouble and whatever you do or tell us stays between us. All we want to do is find our people."

Phoenix took a look at her unit. The men were relaxing, all of them silent and staring at the endless ocean. Although each man had an automatic weapon over their shoulder, it appeared as if they thought they were on vacation. Their fatigues were neat and freshly laundered, and she wondered how long they would stay that way. The temperature was already rising as the sun broke over the blue horizon. Alex and Justin had pulled their caps down over their eyes for some rest while Darius was letting his hand dangle in the warm water. The doctor, Max, was sat cross-legged at the back of the boat, fidgeting with his pack. He was probably not used to carrying one, but he had to pull his weight. They all had their fair share to carry. He was the only one without a weapon, although she saw no reason why they would need them. It was purely a precaution. Max was a doctor and carried a medical kit, mostly for his three colleagues. The assumption was that they were hurt, unable to get off the island. She wasn't sure what they would find: broken legs, arms, or worse?

"Keep your arms and hands inside the boat at all times." Freddy turned around to look at Darius. "Please?"

"What's the problem?" asked Darius. He splayed his fingers and let the saltwater splash up his arm. "You said it yourself, this place is beautiful. We're not expecting company, and I don't see any other ships or boats close by."

"It's not the ships you have to watch out for, it's the sharks."

Darius withdrew his hand quickly.

"See? Beautiful and dangerous," said Karl chuckling.

"No one said there'd be sharks," muttered Darius as he rolled up his sleeve.

"Freddy, what else can you tell me?" Phoenix tugged her cap down over her hair. The sun was blossoming now and they were heading almost directly into its path. She assumed that Freddy must know the ocean well as they were now so far from the atoll that there was no sight of land in any direction. He could be taking them anywhere. There was no computer or GPS to direct him, and he was evidently being guided by his own nose. "Is the island close?"

"Not far. We'll see it soon."

"And you can take us to where you dropped them?"

"Yes, I'll get you to the same place. There's a small cove on the eastern side that is sheltered and quiet. The coral is shallow, and I'll be able to get you nice and close, although your feet will get wet."

"What's the island like?" asked Phoenix.

"I can't tell you with one hundred percent certainty because I haven't been on it. Nobody has. Sometimes we visit just to ensure it is still okay and our ancestors are not disturbed, but we remain on the water in the boat. It is *their* island. My tribe merely ensures it is protected. Their spirits roam freely among the trees and caves. If you could hear them, they would tell you everything you wanted to know."

"Yo, Alex." Justin shoved Alex in the ribs. "You still talk to dead people? We need your skills, man."

"Fuck off." Alex leant back in the boat and closed his eyes.

Phoenix ignored them and hoped Freddy hadn't heard. "Can you tell me what sort of vegetation the island has? Is there a water source? What about animal life? Are there fish, mice, birds, anything at all?"

"You will see very soon. We are almost there. I'm not sure about the animal life. Birds, certainly. This whole area is a mecca for seabirds. But I have never ventured inland. The beach is as far as I have gone. It would be disrespectful for me to tread any further without being invited."

"By your ancestors?" asked Karl. He snorted. "I don't take orders from dead people."

"No, by my chief," replied Freddy brusquely. "He is the only one with the authority to allow you onto the island." Freddy sighed. "There is a certain way of doing things out here that you might not understand or care for, but that is the way of it. We have rules and I am not comfortable with you being on our island. I understand why you want to go, but really, I am not sure about this. You have your guns and attitude that will upset the way of things. I do not wish for my people or land to be disrespected. Perhaps I should—"

"No, please." Phoenix got to her feet. Karl was pushing Freddy's buttons, none of them good. She could sense that Freddy was about to turn the boat around. He was their only way in, the only chance they had of accessing the island. She put a hand lightly on his arm. "There are three people depending on you, Freddy. They're relying on us to save them. Please. We won't cause any trouble. Give us the day and then we'll be gone. You won't even know we were here."

Freddy pursed his lips. "Yes, okay, okay. I feel bad for those people. They were nice. All of them were very friendly to me and my tribe."

"Yeah when they got their cheque-book out," muttered Karl. "I always find people friendly when they're paying for something."

Phoenix turned to face the boat. "Squad Leader Walker, ready your men. I want a full weapons check. We are approaching unknown terrain, possibly hostile. This isn't a vacation and your thoughts are not required at this time. Quite frankly, your unit looks like they're on a fishing trip, not a rescue mission. Pull your men together, or you'll soon find that this day is going to get a lot worse for you. I would hate to have to tell General Greene about how my squad leader's lack of cooperation jeopardized the mission."

Karl slowly stood up and looked at Phoenix. "Ma'am."

As he ordered the rest of the unit to attend to the weapons and get their gear in order, Phoenix turned back to Freddy. "My unit is under a lot of pressure. Please ignore them. We're on your side on this. We just want to get our people out of there as fast as we can. You can appreciate that going into the unknown like this is a little unnerving for my men."

"Of course." Freddy steered the boat away from the sun and throttled down the engine. "I take responsibility for them. I left them there, and when they didn't return, I was unsure what to do. I hope you can find them."

"You're not coming on the island with us?" Phoenix had to admit she wanted Freddy with them. He would know more about the island than anyone.

"No, I will return to my home after I've dropped you off. I'm sorry, but I have work to do. It would be wrong for me to go onto the island without my chief giving me the proper authority. There are certain protocols to follow. I want to help you find those three people, but it is best if I wait for you. I understand you will be back before evening?"

"Yes. As soon as the sun goes down, we'll head back. This is not an overnight operation. We'll find them before then."

As Freddy slowly turned the boat to the west, suddenly the island came into view. Phoenix had imagined it to be little bigger than the atoll they had landed on earlier, yet the island was huge. How could something so large be uncharted or uninhabited? She estimated that it was a couple of miles across and at least the same in depth. There were low-lying rocks and cliff faces scattered across the lower edges of the island and white sand dotting the coastline. Small coves and bays where the blue ocean lazily drifted across the coral looked inviting, like postcards from paradise. In the center of the island rose a sharp cliff, lush vegetation growing all over it. She guessed it might be an extinct volcano. If so, then the soil would be full of minerals which would explain the rich plant-life and trees that seemed to cover almost all of the island. The ocean surrounding it was a rich, dark blue and yet the sky above it much lighter. There was no hint of a cloud forming, just endless azure blue that lifted her mood. She was worried about the mission, about what state they were going to find the three people in, about Karl's attitude rubbing off on the men, and yet as she looked at the island, she felt a peace settle over her.

"Beautiful, right?" Freddy grinned. "This place is sacred. It is the home of our forefathers. They lived here once, many years ago, before moving across the oceans and colonizing the other islands of the Yasawas. This was where it all started. They left this place to explore, to tell the world of its beauty."

"Ready, Staff Sergeant."

Phoenix looked at Karl. All of the men were ready, and despite Karl's growing irritation, he was ready too. The doctor was still at the back of the boat fanning himself with a cap. He looked pale and sweat ringed his armpits.

"When we get to the island, make sure Max is okay. He looks a little seasick."

"Ma'am."

The little boat began to slow down, and Freddy drew them closer to the island. Up close it looked formidable, its central peak dark and harsh against the blue sky. The white sand beaches were pleasant to look at, but Phoenix sensed they weren't as inviting as they looked. There were jagged rocks surrounding many of the inlets, and the thick vegetation sprang up quickly once the sand gave way to volcanic soil.

"Karl, you brought the machetes, right? I think we'll need them."

"Justin? Show 'em to me," ordered Karl.

"I assume you don't mean my tighty-whities." Justin pointed out two wooden handles beside him, the long blades covered in a flimsy cloth. "I would prefer a flame-thrower, but I guess these will do."

"Shotgun," said Alex as he picked up one of the machetes. He ran a hand over his shaved head and held up the machete. The sun splintered as it flashed over the blade. "It's blunt as fuck, but I can handle it."

"You're a regular Michonne aren't you, Alex?" laughed Justin. "Only without the dreadlocks."

"Fuck you, Justin. I used to help my pop when I was a kid. We had the biggest ranch for a hundred miles. I know what I'm doing." Alex slid the machete back down the side of the boat carefully. "Anything gets in my way and it's off with its head."

"Okay, wind it up, we're here." Phoenix looked nervously at the island. She had no doubt in the ability of her unit, but it felt surreal. Approaching the island felt like she had gone back in time, to when the oceans were uncharted and islands were still uninhabited.

"How come nobody found this place and built a Hilton resort?" asked Karl. "Your tribe could make a lot of money out of a deserted paradise island."

"It is more important to us to protect the island. There is no price that would separate us from our spiritual home. Would you sell your graveyards in America? Would you build a hotel over a sacred place?"

"The fact that you're even asking that question shows you don't know much about America, Freddy." Karl stared at the island. "There's a price for everything."

A lone seagull took off from a nearby beach and cartwheeled overhead before flying out to sea. They were heading for a small bay fringed by long grass and bushes sporting small yellow flowers. As Phoenix peered over the side of the boat, she saw the coral only a few feet below. Small fish swam around, their bodies a fascinating hue of blues and purples. A turtle bobbed its head up and then disappeared beneath the surface of the shallow ocean again. A large fish with red-and-yellow vertical stripes swam up to the boat and then hurried beneath a piece of coral. A silver fin splashed above the surface of the water and then slipped silently away. Phoenix couldn't quite believe that General Greene had sent them here. The operation would probably be over within a couple of hours. Perhaps the three employees of Space54 had given up on western civilization and decided to set up house on the island. It was an appealing prospect. If there were fruit trees somewhere on the island and a fresh water source, then there was no reason why they couldn't survive. There would probably be mangos, papaya, and coconuts, and evidently there were enough fish to eat if they could be caught.

The engine cut out, and Freddy steered the boat silently to the shore. They were abruptly sent into shadow as the sun hid behind the island's central peak. The air turned cold and Phoenix looked at the island with fresh eyes. It would get freezing cold at night. There was no help if anything happened. The place could be hiding poisonous spiders, scorpions, and snakes. Was the island the idyllic paradise that it looked? On the surface, it was secluded beaches and glorious sunshine. Scratch beneath though and the harsh reality of life would appear. Phoenix watched Freddy throw the anchor overboard, and she felt for the gun nestled at her hip.

Freddy flashed her a smile. "We're here."

CHAPTER 4

"Darius, get off your ass and help the man," said Karl as Freddy clasped two curved pieces of metal over the lip of the boat. With Darius' help, Freddy lowered the gangplank over the side of the boat and then dropped one end into the water. The far end of it was submerged but still visible in the fine sand beneath the clear water.

"Ladies first," announced Darius as he helped Justin over.

"Watch your step, Darius, I'd hate for you to fall in."

Alex followed Justin down the gangplank into the shallow water that rose to their shins, and Max followed behind them clutching his pack to his front. Karl watched his men file onto the island, their boots sinking into the soft wet sand, and then joined them. He could hear the complaints starting about the heat and the flies that were already swarming around them. Suddenly, the operation didn't feel quite as easy as expected.

"Exactly how alone are we out here?" asked Phoenix as Freddy watched the men leave his boat. "How far is help if anything happens?"

"I have the radio that Karl gave me, but I'm not sure it'll work at home. I have to leave now, but I'll be back before sundown. After that, I must get back to my home. It is too dangerous to be out here at dark."

"If you have to, you'll get help, right?" Phoenix watched Alex and Justin on the beach wave their machetes around and make lightsaber noises. "If for any reason we don't make it back here by nightfall, you'll contact the military or Space54. Somebody?"

Freddy shook his head. "I'm sorry. I cannot risk bringing anybody else here. This place means so much to my people.

You're lucky you're even getting a shot at this. I'm sorry, Phoenix, truly, but this is a one-off. *Be back before the sun sets.*"

Phoenix knew she couldn't ask anything more of Freddy. He was already risking himself bringing them here. He felt responsible for the disappearance of the three scientists but ultimately this wasn't his problem. She knew they were on their own. There was no reason for her to think that they were going to encounter any trouble, and every reason for her to think they would pick up the three stranded Americans and be back in time for supper. Yet she was worried. Now that she was actually here, there was something about the island that made her nervous. It was too easy, to picture-postcard perfect; and if something appeared too easy, then it usually was.

"I suppose swimming is out of the question?" Phoenix looked at where they had come from, a never-ending vast expanse of blue.

Freddy raised an arm and pointed south. "Viwa is that way. Waya Island lies to the east. The currents are too strong and the islands are *too* far. You would never make it. Please, don't even think of trying. I wasn't joking about the sharks," he said dryly.

"Thanks, Freddy." Phoenix held out her hand and he surprised her by taking it with both hands. He looked at her intently.

"*Be careful.* I want to take you all away from this place before the sun sets today. The spirits here get restless when they are disturbed. I heard sounds the last time I came here that I do not want to hear again." Freddy noticed the concern behind Phoenix' eyes. "Just be respectful to the island and you'll be fine. I mean it when I said I want to get you all home today."

Phoenix looked at the beach. Karl was ordering her unit to line up and instructing them how best to find their targets, giving out orders, and barking at Darius to quit playing with the machete. She looked back at Freddy.

"Even Karl?"

Freddy smiled. "Even Karl. I'll wait as long as I can."

Freddy let go of her hand and Phoenix turned away. She quickly descended the gangplank and felt the warm ocean lap at her legs. Her feet sank into the sand and she began to wade up the beach to dry land. She heard the engine rumble into life behind her and reached dry sand. The mission was the only thing she could afford to occupy her mind. Freddy had been a pleasant distraction, a welcome one, but that was all he was. Her unit and the three missing people were her priorities now. That and getting everyone back home safely.

"Time to go, Staff Sergeant," yelled Karl.

Karl was standing next to Max who was looking decidedly better now that he was on dry land. Some of the color had returned to his cheeks and he was talking to Alex animatedly about something. Phoenix understood that Karl had got the unit ready, but he also needed to know that he was second-in-charge. His time for leading hadn't quite come yet. Phoenix risked a look back over her shoulder. She had no doubt that Freddy would wait for them as long as possible. She also knew that if they didn't make it back, then there was nothing else he could, or would, do. There could be no mistakes; the operation had to be over by sundown or it was curtains for them all. She turned back to the others. Karl had already got Darius and Justin hacking away at the tall grass leading into the island, and Alex was helping the doctor carry his pack. They were still deep in conversation. She glanced up at the blue sky. They had enough water and rations for the day, but that didn't mean it was going to be easy.

"What's got into Max?" asked Phoenix as she approached Karl. "He and Alex seem to have gotten into something heavy. Some kind of argument about where our three missing people are? Or what kind of animal and plant life we might find on this deserted island?"

"Hardly," replied Karl. "It's Wars versus Trek. Alex found out our doctor thinks Trek is superior, whereas he's firmly with the Jedi. Don't ask me. I just want to get this damn stupid operation over with."

"I'll agree with you on that one. Freddy's made it clear we have to be back before the sun sets. After that, he's gone, and so is our ride back to civilization."

"Copy that." Karl grimaced as he stepped forward alongside Phoenix. It was eerily quiet. If there was any animal life on the island, then it was far away from them. Perhaps that wasn't unusual in itself. They were on an uninhabited island not used to receiving visitors. The birds and rats and bugs would be jittery around humans; inquisitive maybe, nervous definitely. Karl looked across the treetops that fringed the beach, but there were no birds.

"What do you think, Fifi, you really think this place is deserted?"

She shrugged. "I don't really care. As long as we get what we came here for."

"You know I did a little reading up about the Yasawas on the *Reagan* before we left. Their tribes used to war with each other. It was territorial. Sounded like there were cannibals too. It was real primitive stuff."

"Freddy never mentioned anything about that."

"He wouldn't, would he?" They reached the beginning of the jungle and began to follow the path that Darius and Justin had carved through the long grass and weeds. The beach and the muffled waves of the Pacific Ocean cresting over the coral quickly disappeared. The sun blinked out of existence beneath the thick canopy above them, and their idyllic island rapidly transformed into a thick sweltering jungle.

"I know you like the guy, Phoenix, but there's a chance that he could be leading us into a trap. I've heard about these places. You know, remote tribes cut off from the outside world for centuries. Along comes the white man and out comes the cooking pot. Tourism only opened up here a few years ago. These people have been separated from the outside world for a long time."

"Save it, Karl, you're not selling me on that one. Cannibals? You think that's what happened to Ricardo, Jane, and Tobias? That they ended up being spit-roasted and eaten for dinner with a side salad?"

"I'm not saying anything." Karl brushed aside the low-hanging leaves of a tree. Ants scurried across the broad palms, ignoring the intruders. "I'm just saying we have to be on our guard and ready for anything."

"Right, Karl. The first sign of a cannibal, I'll be sure to let you know. For now, let's focus on keeping up with the others and finding what we came here for. Oh, and if you call me Fifi again, I'll cut your balls off and roast them myself."

Karl looked at Phoenix and stopped. She pushed past him and kept her eyes on the track ahead. Sweat had begun to form on her brow and temples, but she could see Alex's back and wanted to catch up with the others. She wasn't sure if Karl was just trying to wind her up or if he seriously thought there might be a lost tribe living on the island. Just when she thought she liked him, he came out with some garbage. Perhaps he had seen how she had looked at Freddy and was just trying to spook her, to convince her that Freddy was just playing them. Either way, she didn't want to waste any more time on Karl's games. She wasn't about to fuck up her career now and let Karl take over. She picked up the pace and left Karl behind her. She could hear his footsteps, but he had gone quiet. At least he knew when to shut up.

"Alex, how's the doctor?" Phoenix managed to get alongside him and saw that Max was a few feet ahead. "He puke?"

"No, he was just seasick. He's okay now. Although if you'd heard what he'd said about George Lucas, you would think he was insane. Can you believe he—?"

"Can it. I don't want to hear it. You got all your provisions?"

Phoenix glared at Alex. She'd had enough of boy's games and locker room talk. She knew when to lay down the law and when to let her unit relax. Now was not the time for relaxing. Ever since they had learnt of this operation, they had treated it as a joke. It was time to take it seriously and realize that people's lives were in the balance. She had no problem telling them to suck it up. She had seen enough action and done her duty to know when to let them have it or back off. Growing up in Oklahoma with two sisters molly-coddled by middle-class parents hadn't softened her. In fact, it had the opposite effect and had driven her to accomplish something, to do better than her sisters. She didn't begrudge them their comfortable lifestyles, but she had needed to break free, to do something more. That drive was still in her, and she called on it when she needed to. Now was one of those times. Star Wars and cannibals? They'd all spent hours on planes and boats recently with nothing to do, and now that they were here on the island, they still didn't seem to understand what was at stake. The heat was already beginning to suck the strength out of her, and she did not want to spend all day fighting the jungle as well. It was time to pull it together. She let Karl run her unit with a loose lease. It was time to pull it tight.

"Well?" she barked.

"Yes, ma'am. I've got the doctor's too. Thought it might help him, given how he was feeling sick."

"Good. Stick to him like glue. Anything happens to him, I'll leave you behind." She could see from the look in Alex's eyes that he thought she meant it too. "And cut out the chatter. Start looking for signs of our targets."

Phoenix knew she had been harsh on Alex, but he would get over it. She quickened her pace and overtook the doctor. She checked that he was okay, and he confirmed it with a grunt, so she sped past him. There was little to talk about with Max until they found the survivors. Before arriving on the island, she had thought of them as victims, as if they were going to simply retrieve the bodies. Yet she felt energized now that she was here. She began to believe that perhaps they were alive. If they had found water, then there was no reason to think otherwise. Until they found the bodies, then she would continue to believe that they were alive.

"Justin. Darius. What's the deal?" Phoenix found the two men hacking away at more long grass. It fell away in great clumps under the blades, but the pace was slowing.

"This grass is a bitch," said Justin. He turned to Phoenix, and she could see the sweat pouring down his face. His skin was bright red, though still nothing to match his hair. His energy and enthusiasm rarely waned, as if he wanted to prove himself and Phoenix sensed he was enjoying this. A boy's adventure out in the jungle.

"So, who figured out where our three missing people are?" asked Phoenix.

"Come again?" Justin looked at her blankly.

"Well, I assume you're not just hacking at that grass without a good reason to. Are we blindly wandering around this island or have we got a concerted plan on how to find them?"

"If I may?" Max approached Phoenix.

"What is it?"

Max bit his lip and looked at her. "Well, I discussed with your men that the best way of finding our people was to find the downed probe. That *is* what they came here for. It's reasonable to expect that they would head for it too. It seemed like the best place to start."

Phoenix put her hands on her hips and looked at the doctor. "I thought you didn't know where it was?" Max seemed earnest about finding his colleagues, but she was beginning to think that Karl was right. He was just a tourist getting in their way.

"Well, not exactly," replied Max nervously. "But we did have some intelligence that suggested it was somewhere near the center of the island."

"And if they found your missing probe, Max, then what? They obviously didn't make it back to shore, so where did they go?"

"To top up their tan?" muttered Darius.

Max swatted a fly away from his face and looked blankly at Phoenix. He had no answer. "Well, they would have tried to…to get back to the boat. After retrieving whatever they could then—"

"Then what?" Phoenix looked around her unit. They were all staring at Max, waiting to hear what he would say. Justin and Darius had taken it upon themselves to follow his orders and Phoenix had let them. She had conjured up an image in her mind of finding the three missing people waiting for them in a clearing. She had thought that Max might know a lot more than he was letting on, perhaps even where the probe was and where to go, but he was as lost as they were. If they weren't careful, they would be wandering around directionless, a situation that was too dangerous to allow happen.

"*I* don't know. That's your department."

Phoenix looked up at the green canopy sheltering them from the morning sun. There was almost no breeze beneath it, just the hum of invisible flies and humid warm air that made her think she should have followed her sisters and settled for a nice office job with air-conditioning and coffee mornings.

"Right, well in the absence of any clear idea of where they went, the best thing we can do is track them down. We're not going to do that by hacking away at this jungle all day and hoping for the best. We're going to find higher ground. We need to do some recon and figure out where they might have gone, whether they found your probe or not, Max." Phoenix pointed to the island's central peak. It appeared between gaps in the leaves, a formidable-looking rock-face with a gentle green tree-lined slope on one side and a sharp steep drop on the other. "We don't have to get all the way to the top, but we can at least get to a vantage point from where we can get an idea of the layout of the island. We can look for anything unusual from the clearer area where the trees are a bit more thinned out."

"Use the sun," suggested Karl. "Metal objects or anything from the probe may give off a glare or shine in the light. Our three missing people may have erected some sort of beacon or a sign for help. We need to work with this place, not against it."

"It's going to take us forever just to get to the base of the peak." Justin stretched his sweaty back and rubbed his dirty palms together. "Maybe we should split up? If we work in teams, we can cover more ground."

"Not yet," said Phoenix. "We still need to scope this area out before we split up. We stick together for now."

"Back at it then." Darius sighed and began chopping away at a thick bush covered with small pink flowers blocking their path. Vines were draped over it like spaghetti and it was an effort to get through them.

Phoenix grabbed the other machete from Justin and started hacking away at the thick jungle. She knew it was no good to just bark orders. You had to show you were capable and willing to get involved, to do some of the dirty work yourself. Working alongside Darius, they managed to get several yards deeper into the jungle before reaching a small clearing. The area was twenty feet in circumference and there was a dead tree in the center, its roots a tangled mess still half-buried in the ground. The trees around the clearing were tall and strong, and there was no apparent way through.

"Water?" Karl held a metal flask out to Phoenix who took it gratefully.

"Want me to take over?" asked Alex.

Phoenix shook her head. "No, you're with the doctor. Quiz him for whatever information you can get about our three missing people. See if we can build up a picture of what they might have done if they encountered any trouble. Did they have medical training? Did any of them like to go camping? Maybe one was in

46

the boy scouts? Anything that might give us a clue as to their whereabouts."

Alex said nothing, but the disappointment was clear. Phoenix had no time to soothe bruised egos. He would get his turn at the strong-man stuff soon. She had only been using the machete for a few minutes but could already feel the burn in her arms.

"What do you think?" asked Karl as he took the flask off her.

"Darius, hold up." Phoenix told him to stop hacking away at the jungle and called her unit together. "Five minutes, guys. Darius, Justin, take a look around. See if you can find a natural trail through this fucking jungle. At this rate, we'll have used up our water before noon. Listen for any sign of life or running water. Anything at all. Alex, do what I said and give me an update as soon as you can. Max, I want you to tell Alex everything you can about this missing probe and your people. We need to figure out where they are before someone chops an arm off."

The men looked at her and hesitated. "Go on then. Scoot. I'm not standing here handing out ice-creams."

As the men dispersed, Max remained where he was.

"I really think we should head for where the probe came down. It's the best chance we have of finding Ricardo, Jane, and Tobias. I think I can get us pretty close to its location, if you'll just—"

"Not now, Max." The man's face was bright red. He constantly dabbed at his sweating forehead with a kerchief. "Just go with Alex and have a look around. Tell him what you can. Take a break for a minute and get your breath. We're here for your people and we'll find them, but we're going to do it the right way."

"Sure. Okay." The doctor looked downcast and went to Alex.

Phoenix looked at Karl. "I think this is going to be harder than we thought."

Karl reached for the machete. "Well, if it's too much for you, you only had to say. I'll take over from here. Just—"

"I can handle it." Phoenix pulled the machete away. "Stand down. What I mean is this island is bigger than I thought. The tropical vegetation is too thick for us to be chopping it down all day. Maybe this is exactly what our three targets did. Probably got lost, tired, fucked up, and couldn't find their way back to the beach. If we're lucky, we'll find them sheltering somewhere half-starved."

"And if we're not lucky?" Karl took a drink of water.

"Then the beers are on you."

Karl approached the dead tree and kicked it. His boot went through the soft bark and the tree crumbled. He glanced around. Darius and Justin were examining the undergrowth whilst Alex and Max were in hushed conversation on the other side of the clearing. "Cut them some slack. This isn't exactly what we're trained for. Bullets and car-bombs, that's our thing. Remote islands and jungles? I mean, if you're pissed, then take it out on me."

"Please, Karl, spare me. They've treated this whole operation as a joke. I know what you think about us being here and that's fed down to my unit. If they're joking around, then they're not paying attention. That's when accidents happen. I'm just giving them some direction. You know how hard it can be to remain focused out in the field when there's no action. You switch off for a second and you're dead. I need to make sure they are all switched on."

"Okay." Karl shrugged and scuffed his boot on the ground, kicking up the ivy and dirt. He approached Phoenix. "I hear you. And for the record, I *do* think this operation is a joke. You run it how you like. But don't expect me to like it."

"Not a problem, Squad Leader. None of us have to like it, or each other. But we *do* have a job to do."

Karl shrugged. "It's unusual, don't you think?"

"What's that?"

"This clearing," said Karl as he scuffed his feet over the ground again. "I mean, the tree fell down in a storm sometime, right? Judging by how old and dead it is, then must've been a long time ago. But there's no reason for the rest of this area to be so...clear."

"I guess. What does that matter?" asked Phoenix. "Maybe the sun just couldn't get through enough here to make anything grow."

"Maybe. But the whole way here, right from the beach, we've been walking on uneven ground. There have been dead branches and leaves, bugs, all kinds of shit. But look around. There's nothing here. It's as if something flattened the area, as if a bulldozer came through and just squashed it. What if it's the site of an old settlement? Those spiritual ancestors that Freddy talked about?" Karl bent down and began to poke around in the dirt.

Phoenix knew he was right. For once, he wasn't trying to score points. He had noticed something she hadn't. She wasn't sure if it would help them or give them any clue what the hell they were doing on this island, but it was the first sign they had that this place wasn't as pure and simple as Freddy had made out.

"Maybe. But I don't think it's going to help us." Phoenix watched as Karl dug into the dirt and began to pull on something. "Tree root?"

"No, I don't think so."

Karl pulled on what looked like a small branch until it was free from the ground. He stood up and began brushing the thick dirt off it. It was almost eighteen inches in length, and as Karl began to wipe it clean, Phoenix recognized what he had found.

"Holy shit." Phoenix watched Karl wipe it clean and hold it up. "That's a femur bone."

CHAPTER 5

"It's human and it's male," said Max as he turned the bone over carefully in his hands. "Probably."

"Probably? Can you be a little less vague, Doc?" Karl folded his arms. "I thought this was the reason we brought you here. And all you can tell us is *probably*?"

Max stared at the bone. "It's not exactly easy to tell. I'm a doctor. I usually work with *living* patients. You'd need carbon dating and a pathology expert to know for sure. The angle of the neck would suggest it's from a male though. It's not lost any color or degraded, so it doesn't appear aged." Max held both ends of the bone and pulled. "It's strong too. It's not been weathered or subject to any decomposition. Unfortunately, this belonged to someone who only recently passed. I hate to say it, but I suspect it may belong to one of my colleagues."

"Fuck." Justin stared at Phoenix. "This is a fucking waste of time. They're dead. They're all dead."

"Shut up, Private."

"Oh, come on, Karl, you heard the doc. He's holding their bones. They're dead and you know it."

"Painful though it is to agree with Justin, I think he's right," said Darius calmly. "This operation is over. We didn't come here looking for bones. I'm sorry, Doc, but your friends are history."

"We don't know for certain that this belongs to any one of them. It could have been here a while," said Phoenix, noticing the fear on Max's face. He knew it was from Ricardo or Tobias. He didn't want to say it, but she knew exactly what he was thinking. They were looking for ghosts. "For all we know, it belongs to one of the islanders. Freddy might revere this island, but how do we know they all respect it? For all we know, some of the locals come here secretly to fish or party on a Saturday night. This bone could belong to anyone, and until we know anything more, we keep going. This operation isn't finished until I call it."

"So, what now?" asked Karl. "Are we looking for three bodies?"

"Nothing's changed," replied Phoenix firmly. "I want everyone examining this clearing for more evidence. *If* this bone belonged to one of our guys, then there could be more around here. We may find more clues as to what happened and their whereabouts. I need you all to look around and tell me the instant you find something."

The soldiers started grumbling but proceeded to look around. Alex and Max began to examine the ground where Karl had found the bone. Alex used the butt of his gun to dig up the dirt while Max used his hands. Justin and Darius separated and searched the trees, pulling apart the low bushes and scrub.

"Karl, walk with me." Phoenix made her way over to the trees. She bent down to the ground and prodded at the base of a tree covered in vines with her gun. Karl bent down next to her. "I'm not comfortable with this, Karl," said Phoenix.

"Tell me about it. We're wasting our time here. You know it and I know it. This is a wild goose chase."

"That's not what I meant. The odds aren't in our favor, I'll grant you that, but there *is* still a chance they're alive."

"I don't think so." Karl watched a giant ant pick up a leaf ten times its size and carry it up the thick trunk of a tree. "I think Space54 has sent us on an errand to pick up its three dead employees. We're glorified pallbearers with guns."

Phoenix looked over her shoulder. Her unit was still looking for clues but had apparently come up with nothing. They were out of earshot and keeping themselves busy, yet Phoenix lowered her voice anyway. "Remember 2009 when we were outside of Mosul? Remember when those bastards had us pinned down outside that mosque?"

"Yeah, of course. I hardly think this is the time to reminisce. That was a bad day—for *all* of us."

"I remember knowing I was going to die. We had been fighting the enemy unit for what, an hour? I remember vividly not just thinking we might die, but that we were going to. There wasn't a doubt in my head."

"You never told me that." Karl rocked back on his haunches. "You told the general that you never stopped believing, didn't you? You told him the unit was all heroes."

"Yeah, but I know when to bullshit, Karl. That's something you still have to learn how and when to do. Politics and bullshit are the same thing, and until you learn how to play the game, you'll never get your own unit. I told the general what he wanted to hear: that his men were always going to come out on top. I told him that I was with the best damn unit the US Army had, that we would've stayed there all week until we had killed every last one of those Arab fuckheads, and that I knew we would win. You think I was going to tell him I pissed myself waiting to die as the bullets whizzed over my head?"

"Truthfully, I thought we were finished too," said Karl quietly. "When Sawyer took a bullet, I didn't think I would see my daughter again. Mosul was a shithole. That whole operation stank. How many did we kill? A dozen, right?"

"Final count was fifteen."

"And how many of us? Sawyer and Travers. The numbers are on our side, but two is still two too many."

"Right." Phoenix slowly stood up. "I thought we were dead. I thought no matter what we did, they were going to get us. The situation was desperate, you know that, and when Sawyer and Travers bit it, I knew I was going to die. I simply *knew* it."

"Phoenix." Karl stood and put a hand on her shoulder. He looked at the unit as he spoke. "Look, nobody blames you for what happened. What we're doing now is nothing like that. This is a cakewalk."

"Right. I get that. But I want you to know, Karl, that I am not leaving without those three people. They are American citizens, and even when the situation is beyond impossible, even when you know you're going to die, then you don't give up, right?"

Karl nodded. "I see. I see it now. You're right."

"So, before we start panicking and running back to the boat, I need you on the same page, Karl. Are we working together on this?" Phoenix looked at her squad leader. Mosul had been just about the worst situation that they had ever been through, and if they could get through that, then he was right. This *should* be a cakewalk. She had to have him on her side though. The unit had their doubts and it was understandable. She could put herself in their shoes and imagine just what they were all thinking. If Karl joined them, then eventually they would turn on her. She had to maintain order and make sure they stuck to the operation. With Karl barking orders alongside her, they might just manage to get through this.

"I've got your back. You know I have. It's always been that way. No matter what I think, I'd follow you back to Mosul if I had to, Phoenix. And trust me when I say that is the *last* place on Earth I ever want to go."

"Appreciate it." Phoenix wiped her brow. Those memories were ones she preferred to keep buried, but they surfaced occasionally. The memory of knowing she was going to die and the feeling of immense guilt when they got away with only two dead would never leave her. "There's something else bothering me, Karl. The bone you found. It was clean. When the doc was handling it, I couldn't see a scrap of flesh on it."

Karl shrugged and hitched his backpack up on his shoulders. "It's just a bone. It might not mean anything."

"Yeah, but the bone was clean. It's as if something had stripped it clean, you know? The flesh hadn't had time to rot. Max said himself that it hadn't decomposed. I believe him when he says that it's not old. The most likely outcome is that it came from Ricardo or Tobias. So where does that leave us?"

"That someone killed them? Maybe Jane was a secret serial killer." Karl pulled gently on a vine hanging from the nearest tree. It held firm, and he looked up at the top of the tree as he contemplated climbing it. If he could, it would save a lot of time getting to higher ground.

"I'm going to disregard your wild theories about Jane. As for someone killing them, well despite what Freddy said, maybe this island isn't as uninhabited as we thought. If they did bump into some unfriendly locals, then that still doesn't really explain why the bone was completely wiped clean of meat."

Karl was thinking more about how he could climb the tree. Discussing the bone he had found held no appeal anymore. "Hm? Bugs. Just bugs. This place is fucking crawling with them," he said swatting a fly away from his face. "They'd eat the shit off my boot if I stood still long enough."

"Karl, it's only been a couple of days. Bugs couldn't possibly strip a human body down to the bone in such a short space of time, surely? What if it was something else, some sort of larger animal? What if it was something big enough to eat every last drop of meat off their bodies?"

"And big enough to create this clearing?" Karl looked around. "You realize this must be twenty feet across. *At least.* No way is there anything big enough to do that. Even an elephant. And no matter what Freddy told you about this place, about how wonderful and sacred it is, there is nothing you can say to convince me there's an elephant out here. There's nothing that can eat a man like you're talking about. Nothing on land anyway."

Phoenix sent Karl a puzzled look.

"Piranhas. But I don't think we have to worry about them."

"Could be something though." Phoenix looked around the clearing. "Don't you think it's odd that there are no animals? Birds, especially. I would've expected to see parrots or seagulls or something. The only living things we've seen are flies and creepy crawlies."

"Don't overthink it." Karl looked up to the canopy high above his head and tried to judge how far it was. "Look, this island is an anomaly. Maybe there is a whole bunch of seals and seagulls around the corner, or maybe there's nothing at all. Maybe we'll run into King Kong, or maybe we'll just go home with mosquito bites from head to toe. Maybe Freddy likes to bring his girls out here and get funky on the weekend, or maybe we're the first people to set foot on this Godforsaken place. Ultimately, it doesn't matter, as long as we get home. I never thought I'd say I miss Guam, but—"

"Me too." Phoenix smiled. "I'm glad you're here, Karl."

"Me?" It was Karl's turn to smile. "Aw, shucks. And I thought you hated me."

Phoenix had talked herself into a circle. There was something wrong about the whole set-up, she just couldn't figure it out. They needed to know more.

"You think the doc is on the level?" Phoenix watched Max pull something out of the ground next to Alex. It was just a dead tree root and he tossed it away in frustration. "I think he's keeping his cards close to his chest."

"I wouldn't trust him as far as I could throw him, but what's he going to do?" Karl pulled on the vine again. He put all his weight behind it, but it stayed firmly in place. "Forget him. He's not interested in finding those people alive. This is about insurance. Space54 just want to protect their reputation. I'll bet they're paying top dollar for our services. They need to ensure they're seen to be doing everything they can to get their people back. He's going to report back that we did everything we could, that they were already dead and couldn't be saved. The CEO will make a big speech and pay the family a couple of million to keep quiet."

"And us?"

"And we go back to the day-job like this never happened. For now, I guess we just roll with it."

Karl put both hands on the vine and pulled himself up off the ground, using the tree's trunk to brace his feet.

"Karl, *what* are you doing?" asked Phoenix.

"Getting a better look," grunted Karl as he hoisted himself up to the nearest branch. It was only a matter of seconds before he managed to get himself on a sturdy branch. "I have no interest in falling and breaking my back, trust me. I'm just going to try and see a little further. Give me five minutes?"

"Karl—" Phoenix watched him begin to climb the tree higher. It must be a boy thing. She knew that he would be up and back in no time, so she turned around to her unit. They were still looking around for clues, their waning interest in the job all too evident. Max was digging furiously at the ground, but Alex appeared to have given up and was sitting in the dirt checking his weapon.

"We done here, Private?" asked Phoenix as she approached them.

Alex holstered his gun and jumped up. "Haven't found nothing, have we, Doc?"

"You haven't found *anything*, Alex." Phoenix looked down at the doctor. He was poking around in the dirt like a schoolboy. "You mean you haven't found anything."

"No, ma'am, dang it, I gone done and ain't not found nothing."

Phoenix let it go. Alex had a glint in his eye and had learnt from Darius that you could get away with being cheeky only so often. She decided that this was one of those times. "I'll save the grammar lesson for another day, Alex. What about you, Doc? Anything?"

Max grunted and looked up at her. "Actually, I think I have something. It's buried deep, but there's something here."

"Another bone?" asked Phoenix optimistically. She instantly felt bad for hoping he'd found another bone.

"Another tree root?" asked Alex sarcastically.

"No, something far more useful," replied the doctor as he finally managed to pull out what he had been digging for. "A radio."

Phoenix watched as Max slowly extricated a battered-looking hand-held radio from the ground. It was covered in dirt, and Max sat back as he pulled it free before immediately brushing it with the loose hem of his shirt.

"I thought you were shitting me when you said you'd found something," said Alex incredulous. "Damn, here, give it to me."

Alex ripped off his bandana, opened his flask, and poured a small amount of water onto it before offering it to Max.

"Good idea," said Phoenix as she watched the doctor use the damp cloth to clean the radio up. She whistled and signaled for Darius and Justin to come over. "We got something."

"It was close to where Karl found the bone," said Max as he carefully examined the radio. "It was just a lucky find. I thought I saw something metallic beneath the surface, just a tiny corner of something."

"Darius, can you get it working?"

Max handed the radio to Darius. He turned it over and studied it momentarily. "It's intact. It might work. Give me a moment."

As he looked at the radio, Phoenix turned to Justin. "You two find anything?"

Justin shook his head and turned up his nose. "Not a thing, ma'am. I've been around this whole clearing with Darius and there's nothing here. It looks like there is some sort of a path over there in the general direction we want to go. The long grass is shorter for several feet at least. It looks like someone may have cut it down, but I can't be sure. The trail just heads into the trees and we didn't venture too far. I don't know where it leads. Apart from that, no sign of life."

"Tell me it still works." Max let Alex help him up. "They had two radios with them. If it works, we can contact them. We might be able to figure out where they are."

"Don't get your hopes us." Darius turned to Phoenix. "This thing is pretty messed up. I need to get into it and clean it out. There's nothing happening with it. I can't get any power. Maybe if I can check the internal wiring, I might be able to get something, but until then, it's as dead as Hillary's presidential run."

"Great." Phoenix suddenly became aware that they were all looking at her and waiting for orders. They wanted to know what to do next. The problem was she wasn't really sure. Until she knew any differently, it still seemed reasonable to head for the island's peak and higher ground. "Okay, let's ship out. Justin, we may as well take that path you found. If it's a dead end, we'll figure it out soon enough. If not, then at least we might save ourselves from wasting energy. I'm sorry, Doc, but it looks like we're drawing a blank here. I can't say if that bone was from one of your team or not, but we're not going to figure it out standing around here with our thumbs up our asses. Darius, keep working on that radio. With any luck, we might get through to whoever has the other one. We'll just give Karl a moment and be on our way. Everyone, drink some water. It's going to be a hard day."

Phoenix looked at Karl. He was thirty feet in the air, and if she didn't know he was there, then he would be invisible. His uniform blended in with the green foliage and only his black boots were visible beneath a huge leaf. She went closer to the base of the tree and looked up at him. "Well, Robinson Crusoe, what did you find?"

Karl didn't answer but appeared to shuffle around and then his face poked out from behind a thick vine. He looked down at Phoenix and grinned. "Nothing. I can't see over the tops of the trees."

"Then what the hell do you look so happy about?"

Karl shrugged. "I like climbing trees."

Phoenix didn't know whether to laugh or cry. "Okay, well time to go. You good to get down? We found a radio and Darius is going to get it working. For now, I want to get to that peak and—"

The ground beneath Phoenix's boots trembled and vibrations crawled up her legs. "What the fuck was that?" she asked quietly. She looked up at Karl, but if he had felt it too, then he didn't give any indication. He was swiftly descending the tree, skillfully using the vines as ropes.

Phoenix felt the ground tremble again. She looked down expecting to see the cause of the unusual sensation running up her spine, yet the ground was just plain, flat, and dirty. Dead leaves had been squashed underfoot, and there was nothing to suggest they were experiencing an earthquake. She cast her eyes around the clearing but nothing was out of place. The dead tree in the center was still there. Alex and Max were drinking from their flasks. Darius was toying with the radio while Justin cleaned the machetes, sharpening the blade with a stone. A single leaf fell beside her, casually touching her shoulder on the way down. It landed silently.

"Alex, you feel that?"

"I ain't felt nothing, not me, not nothing."

"Now is not the time," said Phoenix as she walked toward him. "And remind me to give you a lesson in English when we get back to base."

"Sorry, ma'am. You mean that little shudder? Nothing to write home about."

"Pack up. We're leaving."

Phoenix turned around to see that Karl had stopped. He was ten feet from the ground and staring at her.

"We have a deadline, Karl," she yelled up to him. "Today, please."

Karl raised his index finger to his lips slowly and then pointed above her head, at something behind her.

"What the hell is he doing?" asked Alex.

"I think he's trying to tell us to shut up," said Max. "But what he's pointing at, I don't know."

Phoenix followed Karl's finger and studied the trees. Alex and Max did the same, curious to know what he had seen. Yet the trees all looked the same, just with slightly different shades of green.

"Hey, Darius, you see anything over there?" called out Alex.

Darius looked perplexed. "See what? There's nothing here."

Phoenix saw it. Karl had been pointing at it, but they hadn't been looking high enough. They were scanning the jungle for something, but they should have looked higher. Right at the top of the trees, she saw two blue eyes looking back at her. It was bizarre yet unmistakable; she was looking right at them. The eyes were rather like dish plates, large and circular with black dots in the center. What they were attached to, she didn't know. Whatever it was, the head and the body were smothered in the jungle's foliage. Was it some kind of ape? She remembered Karl joking about an elephant, but right then, it seemed completely plausible. What color eyes did monkeys and elephants have?

"Alex, there's something in the trees over there beyond Darius and Justin," said Phoenix calmly and quietly. She took out her gun slowly. "Take the doctor to Karl."

"For real? I can't see shit." Alex took his gun out and told Max to start walking slowly toward Karl. "What is it?"

"Just go," hissed Phoenix. "Stay quiet and be ready."

"For what?"

"For anything." As Alex and Max walked away, Phoenix tentatively stepped toward the dead tree. "Darius. Justin. Keep your voices down and come here. Quickly."

At the sound of her voice, the two men turned to her and something seemed to shift in the trees. It was as if a breeze had suddenly come up. The vines moved and twisted, and several large deep green leaves shook. There was a faint tremor in the ground, and Phoenix remembered sitting in the bunker outside of Mosul, knowing she was going to die. The ground had shaken then too from the explosions all around her. This was different. Something in the jungle was causing the ground to shake. This was no elephant.

Darius and Justin began to trudge toward her. Darius shoved the radio into his pack and saw her draw her gun.

"What gives?"

Justin carried the two machetes and looked at Phoenix with reproach. "Ma'am, with all due respect, I'm kinda tired of this. It's hot and funky in this jungle, and—"

Phoenix saw the two blue eyes close, and for a second, she lost it. It was like a mirage. The animal in the trees disappeared and then it was back. First its head appeared and then its arms and body. The creature was as tall as the trees, and when it moved, the ground trembled in fear. There was no sound, no warning call or indication it was even there. If she wasn't looking right at it, she wouldn't have known it even existed. Darius and Justin were no more than ten feet away, and completely oblivious to it. Phoenix studied the creature. Her immediate thought was that she had gone insane. What she was looking at didn't exist. It looked like a dinosaur, like the Tyrannosaurs that she had grown up watching in films and reading about at school. Was it really possible she was looking at one now in the flesh?

"What is *that* fucking thing?"

Phoenix whirled around and saw Alex grappling with his gun.

"Jesus Christ!" Alex yelled and pointed his gun at the creature.

"No, don't fire," ordered Phoenix. She was hoping that if nobody made any sudden movements, they wouldn't spook it. She wanted to believe that they could turn around and walk out of the clearing, away from it. They had intruded on its territory, and if they slipped out quietly, perhaps it would let them go. There didn't need to be repercussions. They could all walk away. Phoenix saw the fear on Alex's face, but he hadn't fired. The doctor was cowering behind him and Karl had gotten to ground level. His gun was raised too, aimed squarely at the creature. "Don't fire," repeated Phoenix. "*Wait.*"

She turned around. The thing wasn't looking at her anymore but at Darius and Justin. They had stopped walking and were looking up at it in amazement. It had managed to sneak up on them almost unnoticed, and now they were captivated. This was the moment. This was when it would be decided if today was going to be a good day, or a bad day. She raised her gun and told Darius and Justin to come to her. She had to get them away from it.

As they turned around, the monster opened its huge jaws and uttered a roar that sounded like all the bombs and explosions Phoenix had ever heard in her life sounding at once. It echoed around her head and she dropped to one knee as she opened fire.

"Run, now. Go!"

CHAPTER 6

The ripple of gunfire sparked Darius and Justin into life. They burst into a sprint, running away from the creature as it also sprang into action. Phoenix sensed they were going to be too slow. Considering its formidable size, the monster was evidently light on its feet. Perhaps it had to be to catch its prey. The monster roared again, and Phoenix clambered up onto the dead log. She unloaded her gun and knew the rest of her unit was doing the same. Some of the bullets had to be hitting it, yet it wasn't slowing or stopping. All around her she saw the trees ripped apart, spewing shards of bark and leaves that fell to the ground like downed helicopters. The jungle was torn apart under the constant barrage, and yet the creature kept coming, not caring if it was hit or hurt.

"Justin!" Phoenix yelled at him as he approached. "Toss me a machete and keep running! Get out of here!"

Running at full speed, he threw a machete that landed a few feet short of her. She jumped down off the dead tree and reached for it. The ground was shaking and it was hard to stand, but she grabbed the machete and stood up as Darius and Justin fled past her.

"Let's see how you like this, *bitch*." Phoenix tucked her gun in its holster and charged at the creature. Never had she seen anything like it. It was terrifying and yet magnificent. The thing towered at least seventy feet above her. It had two short legs, full of muscle and power that carried its huge body. Its skin looked similar to a snake's, dark and shiny, and it was covered in a kind of downy fur or feather. It had two upper arms, shorter in length than its lower legs, and each arm ended in three sharp claws. Its head was the size of the boat they had arrived at the island on, and its jaw was elongated, full of sharp teeth.

Phoenix dodged its snapping jaws and sprinted right underneath the creature. As she darted under it, there was a rank smell, a musky odor that reminded her of the time she had found a dead dog with her sisters. It had been hit by a truck and crawled off to the side of the road to die. Its festering, maggot-riddled body had expanded and exploded in the Oklahoma summer heat, and by the time they had discovered it, the poor animal was barely a dog anymore. The smell of that dead creature hit her nostrils again as she got within a few feet of the monster above her. She sensed it trying to stop and turn, and she rammed the machete into one of its legs. The blade penetrated the thing's skin and then snapped. She had succeeded in getting it barely six inches through its thick hide. The machete simply snapped leaving her with nothing but a useless handle in her hands. She tossed it aside and skidded to a halt.

"Phoenix, get out of there!"

She heard Karl yelling and looked back. Darius and Justin had made it to the far side of the clearing. They were lined up firing their weapons and Karl had a grenade in his hand. He wouldn't risk using it while she was in the line of fire, yet there was no way past the thing to safety.

"Move!" yelled Darius.

Phoenix looked up at the creature that had interrupted their operation. In seconds, it had destroyed any notion she'd held that the island was a pristine paradise. The island was more deadly than she had imagined. She had felt something when they had approached but shrugged it off as fear of the unknown. Now she knew better. She tried to catch her breath, aware she was in danger of panicking. When she had been pinned down outside of Mosul, she knew she was going to die. Yet facing this thing that loomed over her and the jungle, she felt different. She was still afraid, and she had no idea how to fight it. But death was far from her mind. She still had a job to do and her unit to protect. She had been wrong before and had to admit she had no idea how this was going to pan out.

"Go," she yelled. "I'll find you. Go to the peak."

There was no way past it. There was no way to fight it. The only option that meant she might live to see another birthday was to run. Phoenix turned on her heels and ran for the jungle. She could sense the monster behind her, charging for the trees. If it beat her, then she would make for a nice snack before it turned and went after her men. She had to make it. Phoenix ran, focusing only on getting to the jungle where she could hide.

As the bullets flew over her head and tore apart the jungle, she felt the ground rumbling. The monster was close. Phoenix didn't look back. She knew better than to waste time looking at her enemy. She ran and made it to the trees, instantly sweeping aside a curtain of low-hanging vines and hurtling into the jungle. Instantly, the sun was blocked out by the thick trees and the ground underfoot became clogged with bushes and greenery. She pushed ahead, forging a rough path. Branches and leaves slapped her face and body as she ran, small bushes and plants trying to trip her up with every step. Her heart pounded as she ran through the jungle, and the sound of the gunfire dissipated with every second. Soon, she had put enough distance between her and the clearing for the sound to stop completely. She risked a look back over her shoulder, expecting to see the giant looming over her, those huge jaws ready to snap her head off. Although she could hear it charging through the jungle and the sound of trees being uprooted, she couldn't see it. She also knew that just because you couldn't see the enemy didn't mean they weren't close by. As she turned her head to look in front of her, she tripped over a rotten log and ended up sprawled out over the jungle floor. Her hands found a wet mulch and the ground was boggy. Had it been harder, she knew she might've broken something or twisted an ankle, so she was thankful for her soft landing. She could take being dirty and wet any day of the week over a broken limb.

Her breath came out in quick gasps, and she knew she had to control her breathing. She forced herself to take shallow breaths and listened. She needed to know if the monster was still coming after her or had returned to the clearing. She was certain that Karl would lead her unit toward the peak and try to rendezvous with her later. As her chest rose and fell, she listened intently to the jungle.

There was no birdsong. There was no rustling of leaves around her. There was only the sound of the monster following her.

"Shit," she said, getting to her feet.

Phoenix had to decide quickly whether to keep running or hide. She wiped her hands clean on a shiny wet leaf and looked around. There were precious few places she could hide. She could try to climb a tree but doubted that she was as agile as Karl. If she got caught halfway up, then the monster would find her and kill her with ease. Would the upper branches even offer much shelter? Phoenix looked around to see if there was anywhere at ground level she could hide. The trees were all healthy and strong, and the trunks were solid. The vines that hung from them would offer a little protection, but would that be enough? Remembering the dead dog, a thought occurred to her that maybe this thing didn't even hunt by sight. What if it could smell her? What if she buried herself in dead leaves and dirt only for it to dig her out using its sense of smell?

A sharp crack not far away told her it was getting closer. Another tree down, another piece of the jungle destroyed. Phoenix took out her gun and checked how many rounds she still had. She still had her pack on her back which contained more ammo, and she had a single grenade too. She could stand and fight. She could wait until it was almost on her and then blow it to hell. The downside to that plan meant she would go with it. As much as the thought of killing it pleased her, she didn't want to join it and die today. After surviving tours of both Iraq and Syria, it felt like it would be an anti-climax to blow herself up on a remote Pacific Island. Phoenix put her gun away and ran.

Instantly, her chest began to heave and her lungs raged for air. She was fit and worked out, but running had always been her least favorite option. She would rather press weights than go for a run. The green jungle flashed by her as she pushed on. Deep green leaves that were so dark they were almost black, and minty green flowers that sprang randomly from the earth. Still, the trees crowded around her and tried to block her way. She wished she still had the machete and wondered if she had even hurt it? Had it noticed it had a large blade stuck in its leg? Phoenix remembered how it had stopped going after Justin and Darius to turn on her, so it must have felt it. Even if it were no more than a mosquito bite it had been enough for it to notice her, and that meant it could be hurt. Phoenix suddenly reached another clearing. It was much like the previous one, only a lot smaller. She stretched out her arms and reached the trees on either side. The trunks were cool to touch. She tried to control her breathing once again and knelt down. The ground here was hard, baked dry by the sun. As she regained her breath, she looked up. Several of the upper branches had broken away leaving a clearing in the high canopy. A patch of blue sky and a hint of sunlight hit her, and she enjoyed feeling the warmth on her face.

"You were right not to come here, Freddy," she said. "But this island is definitely not what you thought."

Phoenix slowly stood and listened carefully. Still nothing. As she listened to the silence, she realized that she couldn't hear anything at all, not even the monster. Had it lost her or given up? She stayed in the small clearing and put her hands on her hips. She screwed her eyes up and listened. Nothing. The creature might be agile, but getting through the thick jungle might not be so easy for something ten times her size and carrying an extra five thousand pounds. Phoenix thought back to when she had run by it. She was going to have to call it for what it was. She couldn't keep thinking of it as a monster. It was more definitive than that. It was a dinosaur.

A laugh escaped Phoenix's lips before she even realized it was coming. Her own voice sounded funny in the silence which only made her want to laugh some more. She was alone on a deserted island with a dinosaur chasing her. Phoenix bent over, coughed, and then laughed again. There was nothing remotely amusing about her situation and yet, as the sweat poured down her body, she couldn't help but laugh. She waited for it to pass and finally got control of herself.

"Well, this is a first even for you." Phoenix had to say it out loud to know she wasn't mad. It was a dinosaur. She was running from an actual live *dinosaur*.

"Okay, Fifi, sort your shit out." Talking to herself was not a common thing for her, but there was something unnerving about being surrounded by the jungle and absolute silence. She needed to hear something or she would begin climbing the proverbial walls; in this case, tall trees. It almost made her wish to be back in the chaos of Iraq surrounded by explosions and gunfire. Almost.

Phoenix knew she had to get back to her unit. Isolated, she was in danger. She had to find the peak, or at least get back on track to it. She couldn't have run more than a mile so finding the others shouldn't prove too difficult. That was assuming they didn't run into the huge dinosaur that wanted to eat them.

"A freaking dinosaur?" Phoenix shook her head. It still took some believing, even though she had seen it with her own eyes, smelt it with her own nose, and stabbed it with her own hands. *She had stabbed a dinosaur.* A hundred thoughts crowded Phoenix's mind at once. What kind of dinosaur was it? How would she find the peak? Was Freddy still waiting for them? Was it a Tyrannosaur or some other kind of dinosaur? Had it killed the others that they had come here to rescue? What would her sisters say when she told them? Just how hot did it get on this island?

Her breathing was now back in control and Phoenix looked around. Everything looked the same. Finding a way to the peak was going to take some time. She couldn't risk going back the way she came so she was going to have to continue on, and then circle back around. She looked for a natural path through the trees and then froze.

There, in the trees, she saw it. Moving so slowly it was almost imperceptible, she saw the dinosaur coming toward her. One of its blue eyes was monitoring her from behind the cover of the trees. Its thick body was inching toward her. The animal was hunting her, like a lion stalking a gazelle.

Phoenix moved her hand toward her gun and wondered if she would have time to get it out of its holster, let alone have a chance to use it. The dinosaur was at the edge of the clearing now, barely six feet away from her. She could smell it again. If it could move its jaws as fast as it could run, then she knew she had seconds to decide. She could shoot and hope for the best, or run. Neither option sounded promising. It was so close that she had little to no chance of escape.

"Fuck it." Phoenix pulled her gun out and raised it just as the dinosaur charged.

The gun went off, hitting the thing's head, but the bullet seemed to bounce off harmlessly. The dinosaur charged forward but caught on the thick trees, allowing Phoenix a moment to turn. She heard its massive jaws snap shut right behind her, and Phoenix darted into the jungle once more. The ground shook and it felt like she was trying to run on a waterbed. Phoenix tried to run, but the jungle was thick here and there was no clear path. She heard the monster snorting and breathing directly behind her and suddenly a tree was knocked over right beside her, landing in her path. She slowed, unsure where to head. The jungle had her trapped. The dinosaur let out a roar and she knew she was cornered. Like a bug flying into the path of an oncoming car Phoenix quickly whirled around and raised her gun. Up close, the dinosaur seemed even larger. Its jaws were so close that she could count each tooth individually. She pulled the trigger, intending to shoot the dinosaur and hoped it might be enough at such close range to scare it off. But before she could even fire, the creature locked together its jaws and swung its thick scaly head from left to right, smashing into her and knocking her off her feet.

Phoenix didn't fly far. Her body smashed against the large trunk of an old helicopter tree surrounded by Sea Derris. She let out a small cry as the wind was knocked out of her and she landed roughly on the ground. Something in her shoulder cracked as she hit the tree and then she curled up into a ball as she lay in pain on the ground. It felt like every bone in her body had been broken, and though her eyes were open, she saw nothing but dizzying gray. Aware that the dinosaur would be coming in for the kill, she tried to stand, but her legs were like jelly. She could still see nothing and when she attempted to get up her head spun. Blood seeped over her lips and she ran her tongue over her teeth, finding a gap where one of her premolars used to be. Phoenix put a hand on the base of the tree and desperately tried to breathe. Sucking air into her lungs was painful, and she suspected she had a broken rib or two to go with her shoulder. The gray swimming around her vision faded and she began to see dark shadows and greens. She looked up to see the dinosaur casually walking to her. It took giant strides full of aggression and confidence. This was the king of the jungle;

there was no doubt about that. Did it see her as food or just an amusing plaything?

Reaching for her gun, Phoenix realized she had lost it. It was somewhere between her and the monster. She had dropped it when it had knocked her off her feet. It was gone.

"Fuck you." Phoenix spat a lump of bloody phlegm out and raised herself up, wheezing and coughing. Her backpack was still on and she reached around slowly, keeping eye contact with the beast approaching her. "You want to play? You think I'm going to roll over and let you do whatever you want?"

Phoenix slipped one hand around her back and pulled out her grenade. If someone had offered her a bet on whether they would find a use for it on the island, she would have laughed them away. This was supposed to be a simple rescue operation. This was supposed to be a tropical island full of coconuts and colorful fish. The grenade was cold and hard in her hand. Searing pain was rushing from her shoulder to her neck and into her brain. "Fuck you. You want to eat something? You want to eat *me*? I'll give you something to eat."

Phoenix pulled the pin. She pulled her arm back to throw the armed grenade right at it, but as she did so, the dinosaur broke into a run. It charged like an angry rhinoceros. Phoenix's eyes widened as she saw its huge crushing jaws widen and she knew she was going to die. It wasn't going to be a bullet from a sniper or from friendly fire like some she'd known. It wasn't going to be from old age or a drunk driver coming home from a late-night party. She was going to be eaten by a fucking dinosaur. Phoenix closed her hand around the grenade. If she was going down, then she would take it with her. One bite of her would be explosive. At least she knew her unit would make it off the island alive. She thought of closing her eyes, but she wasn't scared of dying. She wanted to look into the eyes of her killer.

At the last second, the dinosaur clamped its jaws firmly shut and swung its head again. Phoenix suddenly realized it was still toying with her and she braced herself for the impact. Its thick skull caught her in the side once more and the world turned upside down. The jungle and sky merged as green and blue flashed across her eyes. Branches and leaves whipped her face, opening up her skin like soft butter. Her arms flailed, reaching for a hold of something, but the vines were flying past her too fast to get a grip on. The grenade slipped from her hand and dropped to the ground. The dinosaur fleetingly appeared in her vision as she flew above it. The creature was watching her, its blue eyes giving only a hint of satisfaction as the dinosaur played with its food.

Phoenix began to scream. Her body slammed up against another tree, this time several feet off the ground. She began to fall and crashed through the lower branches and vines. Something else snapped inside of her, and when she landed in a crumpled heap at the base of the tree, she forgot all about going home. She forgot about seeing Karl or her unit again. She forgot about trying to rescue the three people they had come here for. She wanted to die. Her left arm was blazing in agony and her mouth was full of blood. Phoenix looked up. Her left eye was useless, swollen and bruised. Through her right eye, she saw the dinosaur walking toward her again, brushing aside the jungle and trampling anything in its way. It wasn't going to stop until it had battered her into oblivion. It would break her body over and over until she was nothing but a jellyfish. *Then* it would eat her. All it was doing right now was playing with her, tenderizing the meat.

A tear fell from her eye and she slumped over. Dying was more horrible than she thought. It wasn't quick. And it really fucking hurt. At least out in Iraq she had been surrounded by her unit, by people who cared and would fight for her. Out here in the jungle, alone, scared, she felt sorry for herself. It wasn't fair to go like this. It wasn't right. She lay on the ground waiting for it, waiting for those prehistoric jaws to snap her in half. At least then the pain would stop.

And then she felt it. Another tear fell from her eyes with the knowledge that this was her final breath. Warmth enveloped her quickly, spreading over her body like a soothing blanket. She was lifted up into the air, her body as limp as a rag doll. There was no pain, just a deafening roar and then the sensation of flying. She waited for the sharp teeth to tear into her or for the dinosaur's head to smash into her again, but this time was different. She opened her good eye and heard another roar. She saw flames all around her, orange and red turning the jungle into a flaming fireball.

The grenade.

Phoenix smiled, exposing a row of bloody teeth. She had forgotten what she had been holding in her dirty hands only moments ago. The grenade had exploded close by, enough to send her into the air for the third time in the last few minutes. The dinosaur had been close, certainly close enough to have felt the impact of it. She didn't know if it would be enough to kill it, but at least it knew she wasn't completely helpless now. She hoped she had hurt the son of a bitch. She hoped she had taken off an arm at least.

As the flames licked at her, Phoenix closed her eyes. She couldn't take anymore; let the jungle take her. She would either burn to death or her body would end up wrapped around another tree resulting in a snapped spine. As the ground rushed up to meet her, Phoenix closed her eyes. The force as she landed knocked the last bit of air from her body and blackness replaced the orange and dark shadows. Finally, Phoenix found peace.

CHAPTER 7

"Bullshit. Freddy's ancestors didn't leave this place to explore. They were escaping. They were running for their lives, trying to get away from it. They probably invented the whole thing about it being a sacred place to scare people away." Justin splashed his face with cool water. "Fucking dinosaurs."

Since leaving the clearing, they had trudged through the jungle for a mile or so before coming across a waterfall. It cascaded down into a lagoon, and the water was pure and clean. The jungle was behind them and ahead lay a much more manageable landscape. The trees thinned out and there was no need to hack their way through any tall grass. The ascent toward the peak was gentle and just being able to see the open sky again was a relief. They had stopped to figure out how to find Phoenix and discuss what they were up against.

"I'm telling you, Justin, it's not a dino. It can't be. Think about it logically. It *can't* be," said Alex.

"Does it matter?" asked Darius. "Whatever it is just handed our asses to us on a plate. You see that thing go down? You see it show any sign we even clipped it? Now Phoenix is out there somewhere. We can't leave her alone with that that thing running around."

"Copy that." Justin rubbed his eyes. "This is so fucked up."

"All right, just take a fucking chill pill and settle down, the lot of you," ordered Karl. "You've got five minutes while we figure this out."

"How are we supposed to chill out with a dinosaur on our asses?" Justin bent down to the lagoon and cupped his hands. He drank some of the water and tried to cool down.

"I told you," said Alex quietly, "it's not a dinosaur."

"The hell it isn't." Justin prodded Alex with a sharp finger. "What do you think it is, college-boy? Huh? What's your explanation for what just happened?"

"Look, dinosaurs were wiped out millions of years ago. It must be a mutation of some sort. Perhaps a Komodo dragon or monitor, perhaps a type of Pacific lizard that, in isolation, has grown beyond its normal size." Alex looked at Darius for back-up. "It's just a freak, right?"

"*You're* the damn freak, Alex," spat Justin.

"I think a spade's a spade," said Darius calmly. "If it looks like a dinosaur, and smells like a dinosaur, then it's probably a fucking dinosaur. Hell, I don't know and I don't rightly care." Darius held his gun aloft. "What I do know is that we need some bigger weapons. I want to see if it *bleeds* like a dinosaur."

"Amen. Would be nice to know exactly what we're fighting." Justin looked at Max. He was sitting in the dirt by the edge of the lagoon, paying little attention to the conversation. "What do you say, Doc? We in the land of the lost? This thing a dinosaur?"

Max frowned. "I don't...I don't really know."

"What are you asking him for, Justin? He's just a doctor. He can't help us." Alex sighed. "Leave him be."

"*Leave him be?*" Justin rolled his eyes and sighed. "Am I the only one who fucking gets this? Max here knew *precisely* what we were walking into." Justin began to skirt the edge of the lagoon and headed for Max. "We just walked right into a damn trap. Space54 knew how dangerous this island was and didn't want to endanger their own people so they sent us. Isn't that right? How long have you known about this? How many people have died here?"

Justin grabbed Max by the scruff of his neck and hauled him to his feet. "Well?"

"Hey, I don't know anything about this. I swear," protested Max as Justin pushed him into the lagoon. The water swept up to their knees.

"You know what I think, Doc? I think you knew full well what was going on. I think you've got a hard-on for dinosaurs and led us all here to die. I think you've been having us on this whole time and now you get Phoenix killed."

"Okay, that's enough, Justin." Karl glared at him. "Let him go."

"This motherfucker?" Justin looked at Alex and Darius. They were pissed and he knew he was right. Max had got Phoenix killed and they would all go down with her. "You hear him apologizing? He's done nothing since we got here but complain. I think we need a good old-fashioned witch trial."

"Drop it, Justin. That's an order," said Karl firmly. Max looked scared. Justin still had him in his grip, and Karl knew that Justin was not likely to be persuaded once he got an idea in his head. "We don't know anything for sure, yet."

Justin smiled. "You remember how it used to go, right? If they drowned, they were innocent, and if they floated, they were liars. Something like that. I think it's time we put Max to the test." Justin grabbed Max and pulled his arms behind his back. "Tell me, Max, why did you really bring us here?"

Justin kicked the back of Max's legs and the doctor instantly dropped to his knees, sinking beneath the surface. Justin forced him to bend over, and he plunged Max's head beneath the water. Max began thrashing, trying to twist himself free, but Justin was strong and he held him tight.

"Justin, that ain't right," said Alex. "He's not done anything to us."

"Oh yeah, what about Phoenix?" Justin pulled the doctor up.

"Please," spluttered Max, gasping for air. "I didn't know anything about it. I was as shocked as you."

"Bullshit." Justin plunged the doctor under the water again, holding his head beneath the surface as bubbles began to pop around his legs.

"You've got five seconds, Private."

Justin looked over at Karl to find he had his gun aimed on him.

"Are you kidding me? I'm just trying to get us some damn answers."

"Three seconds."

Justin gritted his teeth and pulled the doctor up. He could see from the look on Karl's face that he was serious. He pushed Max away toward the bank. "Fine. Whatever. It's not like we've never done anything like this before. You know when you're out in the field that you have to do what it takes. Remember Mosul? *Whatever* it takes, right?"

Karl watched as Max scrambled to the shoreline. Alex and Darius helped to pull him up. The shallow water led up to a stony beach and flat rocks covered in algae. "He okay?" asked Karl without taking his eyes or his gun off Justin.

"I'm fine." Max spat and wiped his face. "I'm fine. I understand where you're coming from, but I did not know *anything* about that dinosaur. Or whatever it was."

Karl lowered his gun but kept it in his hands pointed at the water. He matched Justin's stare. "Justin, when I give you an order, I expect you to follow it, do you understand?"

Karl had led the unit away from the clearing reluctantly. He hated abandoning Phoenix, but she was right. They were better to split up and rendezvous with the monster out of the way. Clearly, they didn't have enough firepower to deal with it, so standing their ground would have been suicide. The unfortunate outcome was that he was now in charge. He didn't want to get it this way, but now that he had the unit under his command, he had to enforce the rules and make sure they all knew how this was going to be. Getting Phoenix back alive might just depend on it.

"Do you understand?" Karl asked again slowly, as Justin simply stared at him. "This is not the time to lose your shit, Private."

Growing up in Chicago, Karl had learnt how to handle himself on the streets. He had avoided getting into hard stuff and never gotten caught or a criminal record. If he had, then he probably wouldn't hold the position he did now. The worst it had ever been for him was when his father had taken off, leaving his mother to provide for him and his brother. His mother, an immigrant from Portugal, had worked hard for them. He knew that now, although at the time he thought life had dealt him a shitty hand. It was getting caught shoplifting and a belting from his mother that had set him straight. It had come around when he had turned fifteen, and he had begun to think of what he should do with the rest of his life. If the Army hadn't come along, he might have ended up in the clink with his brother. Luckily, he had seen the light.

"Yeah. I got it," said Justin. The anger in his tone was obvious, but Karl knew it was as conciliatory as he was going to get.

"Good." Karl put his gun away. "Take a look around you, Justin. Think about where we are. Interrogating Max isn't going to change anything, and I believe him when he says he didn't know about the dinosaur. He could just as easily have been killed as any one of us. He's a dumbass, but he's our dumbass, and it's our job to make sure he gets home in one piece. I'm in charge of this operation now, so I want everyone to get their heads together." Karl looked at them all. Alex and Darius, even Max, were looking at him differently. He was no longer their buddy; he was their boss. Was this how he looked at Phoenix? "Refill your water bottles. In no more than three minutes, I want everyone ready to go. Check your weapons. I want to know exactly how much ammo we have. This operation just changed. We're going to find Phoenix, and then we're going back to the beach to catch our ride home."

Max stood up and brushed himself down. His clothes were soaked but would dry quickly in the sun. "But—"

"I don't want to hear it, Doc. You're lucky I didn't let Justin drown you. Quite frankly, I was tempted to do it myself. Nobody is going to question us if you don't make it home, so I suggest you keep your head down and your mouth shut. I just lost the best soldier I ever worked with, and I am not going to endanger any more of these men on a wild fucking goose chase to find your three colleagues. We're going back into that jungle, finding Phoenix, and getting the hell out of here. Any questions, you can take it up with that monster. You value your life, then you'd better take a good strong dose of some shut-the-fuck-up pills."

Karl heard Alex and Darius mutter, "yes, sir," as they began to check their ammo.

"Justin, get the hell out of the lagoon before you catch something," said Karl. He knew he had a couple of grenades in his pack, but that they would be running perilously low on bullets.

After unloading everything they had to ward off the attack earlier, they wouldn't have much left if they ran into it again. They hadn't come prepared for battle.

"That monster probably pisses in it," joked Darius.

"Yeah, well you're drinking it, funny guy," replied Justin as Darius lowered his bottle to the lagoon to fill it.

"Oh, shit."

Justin looked down at the water. It looked completely untainted by anything. The waterfall was gentle, and there was nothing to suggest the dinosaur did anything but drink it. It wasn't salty, so most likely it was just rainfall or a natural spring. After the jungle, the whole area seemed quite pleasant. There were rocks around much of the lagoon and beneath the waterfall there was a small cave. If they had time, he would have gone exploring, but he knew when Karl was serious, and he was right about finding Phoenix. They never left anyone behind. He just hoped there was something of her left to bring home. He felt slightly bad about Max, but not enough to apologize. He didn't trust the doctor, and right now, he was the only one they had to blame for this sorry mess.

"So, what about...?" Justin felt something brush against his leg. He looked down but saw nothing. It could've been a log or some weeds, but the water looked clear. Whatever had brushed up against him had disappeared. He shrugged it off and headed for the shore. "So, what about Freddy? You think he was on the level when...?"

Justin felt his legs whipped out from under him and he shouted for help just before he was plunged into the cool water.

"Justin!" Karl raced into the water. "What the fuck?"

Where Justin had been standing, there was nothing but a few bubbles popping on the surface. Karl reached down into the water, but his hands felt nothing.

"Where is he?" shouted Alex. "Did you see what happened?"

"I didn't see anything, I was checking my gear," said Darius. "Did he go for a swim?"

"Justin, quit playing around, where are you?" Karl hadn't seen exactly what had happened. One minute he was there, the next he was shouting something and disappearing under the water. "Justin, sound off!"

They listened and looked at the lagoon, but there was no sign of him.

"How long can he hold his breath?" asked Darius.

"A minute, maybe more?" suggested Max. "Depends."

"On what?"

Max looked sternly at Darius. "On what pulled him under the water."

Alex waded into the water next to Karl. He had his gun raised. "Sir, where did he go?"

Karl pursed his lips. "If he thinks this is funny, he's got a shock coming. I thought I'd got through to him. I thought—"

Justin's body floated to the surface a few feet away. He was face down and not moving.

"There!" shouted Darius.

Karl and Alex splashed over to Justin's body and grabbed his arms. They turned him over and Justin opened his eyes.

"Fuck, Justin, what's going on?" asked Alex. He looked down at Justin's body and shivered. "Holy fuck."

Alex nudged Karl and pointed at Justin's legs. They were gone. Something had cut them off and there was nothing below his knees. His legs ended in bloody stumps that turned the water a deep red.

"I'm...cold," whispered Justin as they dragged him to the shore.

"Doc, we need you," shouted Karl. "Now!"

They urgently pulled Justin to the edge of the lake and dragged him up onto the stones. Karl looked at his legs as Max bent over him. Whatever had taken his legs had been big. It looked like a shark attack, as if something had eaten them. Karl had seen soldiers out in Iraq who had lost limbs and the sight of blood was something he had unfortunately gotten used to. But Justin was just lying there as if nothing had happened. He wasn't screaming in pain or writhing in agony. He just lay there as the doctor pulled some bandages out of his pack and began to wrap Justin's legs.

"What was it, Justin? What's in there?" asked Alex.

"Tell me what we're looking for, buddy." Darius had his gun loaded and ready. "Tell me and we'll get it for you."

Justin smiled weakly. All his fire and anger were gone. It was as if he didn't care, but Karl knew it was the shock. His brain had made his body go numb to deal with the pain.

"It was a fish. I think. It looked like a…more like a crocodile."

"Relax, Justin, you're doing fine. You're going to be just fine," said Max.

The doctor looked over his shoulder at Karl and shook his head. He resumed working on Justin's legs.

"A fish? Well, what did it look like?" Darius pressed Justin for more information. "Was there more than one?"

"Darius, leave it." Karl put a hand on his shoulder. "Take Alex and watch the water, but do not go in. We don't want any more accidents or surprises."

As Alex and Darius reluctantly left Justin with promises of retribution and began to monitor the lagoon, Max got up and stood beside Karl. They walked a couple of feet away from Justin so that he was out of earshot. A palm tree had broken over the rocks and offered some temporary shade from the burning sun as they spoke.

"How long?" Karl asked.

Max lowered his eyes. The doctor's hands were covered in blood. He shook his head forlornly as he spoke. "Not long. He's lost a lot of blood. I've bandaged him up, but he can't feel a thing. He's gone into shock. I can administer him some pain relief but—"

"Do it. Then let me talk to him." Karl drew in a deep breath. "Thanks, Doc."

Justin was mistaken. Fish didn't do this. There was something in the water, something like that dinosaur, something unnatural. It wasn't a crocodile either. That would have taken him whole and drowned him. Crocodiles didn't snap off people's legs and then let them go. Karl wanted to kill whatever had done this to Justin, and he hoped that Alex and Darius might find it. Perhaps whatever it was hadn't gone far. Perhaps it was still circling, looking for the rest of Justin to feed on. If it resurfaced, then Karl would have a tasty bullet for it. Just how the day had gone this bad was beyond him. Nobody had said they would encounter anything like this. Intelligence on the island was limited, but it was like Phoenix had said at the briefing: they weren't expecting anything worse than sandflies.

He watched Max slip a needle of some clear liquid into Justin's arm. The soldier hadn't said a word in the last few minutes. His skin was pale and his eyes were rolling around lazily as if he was drugged.

As Max got up, Karl bent down and took Justin's hand. He looked into his eyes. "Hey, Justin. How're you holding up?"

Karl squeezed Justin's fingers but got no response.

"He'll be gone in a moment. I made sure he'll feel no pain," whispered Max into Karl's ear.

Karl watched the doctor trudge over to the shade of the palm tree. He sat down on a mossy rock and put his face in his hands. Justin had just tried to kill him, but the doctor was evidently cut up about the passing of another soldier.

"Hey, buddy, you know we're going to get you home, right?" Karl squeezed Justin's cold hand once more. It was limp and wet, and Justin barely seemed to have the energy to look at him.

"Can't...wait," whispered Justin. "Need... a... coffee."

Karl smiled, remembering that Justin grew up in Seattle before joining up. "No problem. I'll buy you a whole bucket of the stuff. Gonna have a beer first though, right?"

"Right." Justin's eyes rolled back in his head to expose blood-shot white eyeballs.

"Hey, Justin, hold onto me, I'm here with you. Hold on, Justin. It's gonna be okay. You hear me? You're going to be okay," lied Karl. He had performed a similar speech when Sawyer had been blown to bits outside of Mosul. His body had been held together by slender pieces of flesh and muscle, and he had died quickly. Justin wasn't even dying because of enemy fire. He had done nothing to deserve this, and it made Karl angry. At least Sawyer had known what he was getting into. Justin was young and still had a lot to offer. Now he was dying on some deserted island for no good reason at all.

"Tell him I'm sorry," muttered Justin.

"Who?" asked Karl. He tried to reassure Justin there was nothing to worry about or apologize for. "You know, whatever it is you can tell them yourself later. Just relax. You're fine."

"The doc. I'm sorry." A thin line of blood escaped Justin's lips and ran down his cheek. "Tell him I—"

Justin's eyes looked up into the blue sky, and Karl watched as his chest stopped moving. Gently, Karl lowered Justin's arm. He clenched his teeth together to stop screaming and then brushed Justin's eyelids. Another of them was gone. Dead. A boy not even halfway through his life was dead. And for what? Karl got to his feet and stared at Justin's body. If they could even recover Phoenix's body, they would have two dead bodies to get back. He was going to have to explain what had happened here, and yet he wasn't sure he could explain it. How was he supposed to say that half of the unit had been killed by prehistoric creatures?

"Alex, Darius, you see anything?" Karl snapped. He took out his gun. "Well?"

"No, sir, nothing," replied Alex. He was standing close to the doctor atop a large boulder from where he could scan the lagoon.

"Darius? You lost your fucking tongue?" Karl approached the edge of the water. It looked as peaceful as when they had first stumbled upon it. It looked like a picture postcard with crystal clear water surrounded by lush green trees, and a gentle waterfall cascading into the blue lagoon. It was deceiving, just like the island. Phoenix had thought it was beautiful, a paradise. Yet it hid dangerous and deadly secrets.

"Nothing. The water's calm. There's nothing here. How's Justin doing?"

Karl saw Darius heading back to him. He had gone around the small shore and seen nothing unusual. Yet Karl knew it was there. Whatever had killed Justin was still there. It had to be. And he didn't want to let it lie. Why should it get away with it? Karl couldn't believe Justin was gone. In the space of barely thirty minutes, they had lost two of their own. Just what kind of island was this? What kind of place held animals that could do this?

"Listen up," said Karl. "Justin's gone. There's nothing we can do for him except catch his killer. Who wants to help me?"

There was silence. Karl knew they were letting it sink in. He also knew that his men would do everything in their power to avenge him. Grief came later. They had experienced death before and probably would again. Right now, he needed them behind him and to understand the gravity of their situation. He looked at Darius who nodded grimly. Karl turned to Alex.

"Fuck. Yeah, I'm in."

"Right. Let's go fishing."

"May I say something?" asked Max. From under the shade of the palm tree, he looked at Karl. "I think it is very noble that you want revenge for Justin, but that will not solve anything. Phoenix is still out there. My three colleagues are still not found. If you hadn't noticed, then the heat is fast approaching intolerable levels and we don't have the time or energy to waste looking for some kind of killer fish. We should stay on track with the operation. That is the best thing you could do for your friend. I'm sorry about Justin, truly. And Phoenix. But nothing you can do is going to fix this. We need to continue the search for my three colleagues and get back to the boat. Anything that sidetracks us might jeopardize the entire operation."

"Alex," said Karl, unable to contain his anger, "put a bullet through the doctor's brain for me."

"Yes, sir."

Max looked up at Alex. "Wait, surely you understand I am right? You can't—"

"Get it done, soldier, then we'll do a little hunting. I've had enough of this shit." Karl removed his pack. "Take him out. This operation is over. He can't do shit for us now. We're better off without him." Karl looked at Alex and winked. It only took a split-second, but Alex caught it. But the doctor didn't know better, that they didn't go around shooting innocent people. If he believed his life was being threatened, maybe he would learn that they didn't want his opinions or ideas. It was his fault they were in this situation, even if he didn't know about the monsters apparently living on the island.

"Please. Stop, I can explain," pleaded the doctor.

Alex pointed his gun at the doctor and aimed. "Sorry, Doc. Unless you got something to tell me, some information that might really help us, then orders are orders."

CHAPTER 8

"Cut that shit out right now."

The voice came from the trees. Alex looked at Karl, puzzled.

"Hold up, soldier," said Karl. There was uncertainty in his voice. Karl bounded quickly across the rocks to the doctor and Alex. "Watch him."

"Who's there?" asked Darius. "Who is it?"

Karl pushed aside some low-hanging leaves and stepped toward the fringe of the jungle. Something was moving inside. He could hear branches being brushed aside. He raised his gun. No more surprises. He wasn't about to let anyone or anything else get in his way. He wanted vengeance. The heat of the sun was burning his neck and sweat poured down his face, but he kept his gun pointed firmly at the jungle. "Step out here. Hands on your head or you'll eat a bullet. *Now*."

"A local?" asked Darius as he ran up to stand beside Alex. "One of Freddy's buddies maybe?"

"I don't think so," said Max, smiling. He had guessed who had arrived with perfect timing.

As Karl watched, ready to pull the trigger, he saw a figure appear through the vines of the nearest tree. She stumbled into the clearing and looked at the lagoon. "You boys done playing or are you going to help me?"

"Phoenix?" Karl rushed forward to help her. "You look like shit."

"Thank fuck for that," said Alex, pleased to see his staff sergeant back.

Darius rushed to help. "We thought you were dead!"

Together, Karl and Darius helped Phoenix to the open rocks close to the doctor.

"What happened to you? We were going to head back in and look for your body," said Karl. "I thought you were history. We heard the explosion and figured you might have taken that thing out when it got you."

Phoenix winced as she sat down. "It's bigger and tougher than us, but that doesn't mean it's smarter. I thought I was finished to be fair. But I got away. I'm not sure how. The explosion must've scared it away. I might have hurt it, but I didn't see. It beat me up pretty bad, but after the grenade went off, I blacked out. When I came around, it was gone."

"Jesus, you are fucked up," said Darius. "But I'm impressed. You went the full three rounds with that thing, huh?"

Phoenix smiled. Everything hurt. She had been sure that she was finished when the flames had exploded around her. Yet she had suffered no more than a few superficial burns and cuts. Her ribs hurt, and she was going to have some colorful bruises to show off. A tooth had come out and she knew she must look terrible. But she was alive. And now that she had stumbled across her unit, she could resume the operation. She was exhausted but had no intention of giving up now. She had been under pressure before and this was just more of the same. The only difference was the enemy: instead of people shooting at them, they had a hungry dinosaur on their tail.

"Where's Justin?" asked Phoenix as Karl handed her a bottle of water.

Karl watched Phoenix drink. She looked terrible, but he had to admit he was relieved she was alive. His short-lived command had been long enough. "He didn't make it," said Karl. He looked at the placid lagoon. "It looks nice, but I recommend you don't go for a swim. There's something in the water."

"That what all the arguing was about?" Phoenix gulped down the water and wiped her mouth when she was done. "I heard you."

Karl felt his cheeks flush. "Things got a little crazy. I guess this heat and my frustration at losing Justin clouded my judgement. I thought... well, I don't really know what I thought. You know we were just messing with the doc. I just wanted to see the old bastard sweat. For Justin, you know? I'm just glad to have you back, Fifi."

"Sure you are. Now help me up." Darius and Karl put their arms underneath Phoenix and helped her to stand.

"Justin. I can't believe it. You said something in the water? Piranhas? Crocodile maybe?" asked Phoenix, looking over at Justin's body. She could see that something had turned him into sushi. "Or is it alligators in these parts?"

"We're not really sure what it was. I guess this island has a lot more secrets than we anticipated."

"Phoenix, are you sure you're fine? What did that thing do to you?" asked Darius. There were scorch marks all over her uniform and cuts across her arms and face. "Maybe you should let the doc take a look at you."

"Oh, so now you think he's worth having around?"

Karl and Darius looked at each other sheepishly. "Look, Phoenix, we were just trying to scare him. We weren't really going to—"

"Save it. And I expect the chain of command to resume now that you know I'm not dead. So, you can stick to ma'am or sir. It's Phoenix when we get home and talk this thing out over a cold beer. Got it?"

"Ma'am." Karl prodded Darius.

"Yes, ma'am."

"Good. Now tell me what happened to Justin while the doc pops my shoulder back in. Then we're good to go."

Karl filled Phoenix in on exactly how Justin had died.

"Hold still," said Max, smiling as Phoenix lay down on the flat rock next to him. "This might hurt."

"Trust me. I can deal with it. Just stop delaying and—"

Max shoved Phoenix's shoulder back in and she closed her eyes. She wanted to scream in pain and cry, but she refused to let it beat her. After what she had just been through, it seemed to pale in comparison. Especially after learning what had happened to Justin.

"Thanks." Phoenix actually did feel a little better. She looked across at Justin's body.

"You want me to attend to some of those cuts?" asked Max. "I should at least get some disinfectant on them." He began to rummage in his pack.

"Leave it," said Phoenix, putting her arm on the doctor's. "Thanks for the help, but I'll be fine. We have more pressing matters to deal with. Pack your gear up, Max."

Max offered a weak smile. "You might have a concussion. I should really check you over. Just to be sure."

"Forget it." For a doctor, Phoenix had to admit he didn't have a very good bedside manner. He said the right things and made the right moves. He knew what he was doing. But there was something missing. Empathy? It felt like he was going through the motions. It was like when she was talking to someone at a party, but their eyes were constantly scanning the room for someone else to talk with. The doctor was like that too, as if his thoughts were elsewhere. She put it down to fear. Seeing Justin die and narrowly escaping a dinosaur attack would be enough to throw anyone off their game.

"And then you appeared. I guess we should wrap Justin up and head back for the beach, right?" asked Karl. "We can probably make some sort of makeshift stretcher out of these vines."

"No." Phoenix took Karl's hand. "Everyone, on your feet and gather round. Justin is staying here. If we can get him on the way back, we will. Of course we will. But there's no point in carrying him to the peak."

"The peak?" queried Alex. "We're still going?"

"Yes, of course. We have a job to do. There are potentially three people out there who are waiting for us, no, *relying* on us. I'm not abandoning them just because we ran into trouble. This changes nothing. We need to be better prepared and more focused. At least we know a little more about this island and what we're dealing with. But the operation goes on as long as I'm still standing." Phoenix looked at Karl. "Clear?"

Karl shrugged. "Sure. As long as we come back for Justin. Alex, Darius, get some of those palm leaves and cover him up, will you? Don't want him out in the sun all day. We'll take him back when we're ready to go."

Phoenix stared at the lagoon. "You didn't see it, Karl?"

"None of us did." As Alex and Darius hid Justin's body, Karl looked at the doctor. He was standing away from the others, his pack on his shoulders, ready to go and looking at the jungle. "You know, I think we've made a big mistake bringing him along."

Phoenix rubbed her shoulder. "Why?"

"There's something not right. I don't like him. He hasn't done anything per se, but...I don't know. Maybe I'm just stressed. This damn heat is getting to me." Karl let out a sigh.

"You're not in Chicago now, Karl," said Phoenix. "Is this really any worse than Iraq? That was hotter than hell."

"Yeah. I guess so. This is different. It's not real. It's like we've been thrown back in time. I don't even recognize half of these plants. Look at that tree over there. Purple flowers growing up its trunk. You ever seen anything like that?"

"Can't say as I have."

"Dinosaurs and giant fish that eat you? This place isn't just home to prehistoric creatures, the whole fucking island is prehistoric. Everything. It's completely untouched. Shit, I know it sounds crazy, but it all feels off. It looks like paradise, but this place is nothing but a diseased shit-pit waiting to kill us all, pick us off one by one."

"Thanks for the uplifting speech, Karl." Phoenix let her lips curl into a smile. "We're not beat yet. We've been in worse places than this. Maybe this place is a throwback. Who knows what we're dealing with. Let's just get on with finding those three colleagues of Max's and get out of here."

Karl whistled. "Alex, Darius, pick your shit up, we're moving out." Justin had been covered up beneath a makeshift grave comprised of huge leaves and some dead vines.

"Say, Darius, you manage to get any joy out of that radio?" asked Phoenix as he approached.

"The thing is busted," responded Darius. "I haven't really had time to get into it, but I don't think it's going to help us any. I'll have another look as soon as I can."

"Okay, well keep working on it. Go and make sure the doctor's ready to go, will you? Karl, go with him. Two minutes, okay?"

Karl nodded and joined Darius.

"Alex, come here." Phoenix watched Darius and Karl head away and put her arm around the young soldier. "How you doing with all this?"

"I'm fine, sir. I mean, ma'am. Glad you're with us."

Phoenix could tell that Alex was lying through his teeth. He was young and full of energy, but he hadn't served with them for as long as the others. "It's okay to not be okay sometimes."

"The doc said something similar. When we left the beach, he said he used to be in the Army. A long time ago. He said this wasn't a job for soldiers and he was sorry we had to come along, but his company didn't know what else to do."

"Really?"

"Yeah, he said it was really important that they got their three colleagues home. Vital to their future, he said."

"Anything else?" asked Phoenix. "Anything else I should know?"

"Well, it sounds crazy, but... but he said that Star Wars sucks."

"Is that so?" Phoenix raised her eyebrows. "Well, then I guess it's up to us to educate the old man."

"All good to go, Staff Sergeant," announced Karl as he came walking up to them next to the lagoon. Darius and Max trailed behind him. The doctor looked pissed off, and Phoenix suspected that Karl had spoken to him.

"Trouble in paradise, Karl?"

"No, ma'am. Everyone knows their role here. We have a job to do. Darius has our only machete so he's taking lead." Karl pointed toward the peak. "We seem to have left the jungle behind us. The land is rocky and dangerous, so we're going to have to watch where we step, but at least we're on open ground now."

"Then let's roll," said Phoenix. "I want to make higher ground within the hour and figure this out. I want everyone watching for signs of that dinosaur. No more surprise attacks. If we see it again, I want everybody ready."

Darius began to march uphill, over the flat rocks and onto the hill that would eventually lead to the peak. The volcanic ground was hard and brittle, a complete contrast to the dense, lush, jungle. The sun was all over them like a rash, and there was no protection from it out in the open. The heat swarmed around them, bringing irritating flies and thirst.

"Alex, let me take your pack." Phoenix realized suddenly that she had nothing. She had lost everything fighting the dinosaur and all the others were still weighed down by their packs. They all had guns too, while Darius had the machete and Karl still had his grenades.

"It's okay, I'll be fine." Alex wiped the sweat from his brow. "I just want to get on with it now."

"That wasn't a question, Private. You can keep your weapon, just give me your pack."

Alex slipped it off his shoulders and Phoenix slung it over her back.

"Don't forget to keep a look out for any sign of our survivors," said Phoenix as they marched uphill. "Any clue as to their whereabouts."

The barren hillside almost made her wish for the jungle. The heat of the sun seemed to hit the ground and rebound up into her face. It was like walking through a sauna fully clothed. The trees had thinned out and were shorter here, as if the sun had made them wilt and stunted their growth. Patches of grass grew sporadically, but it was more like burnt stubble than grass. She looked up at the island's central peak. It was probably another two hundred feet up and the top of it appeared to be completely barren. They didn't need to reach the highest part though, just get high enough that they could get some sense of where they were and look for the survivors. She wanted more than ever to find them now. It would give Justin's death some meaning.

Phoenix looked around. The ocean in the distance was becoming visible through the sparse trees and bushes. It was shimmering under the sun, the calm water looking so cool and inviting that it only made the oppressive heat feel worse. Behind her, the jungle was also becoming clearer. It stretched a long way around the island before petering out into white sandy beaches and coves. It was clear now why there was no resort, why no one from Freddy's village had set up home here. Maybe his ancestors had lived here once but that was a long time ago.

Phoenix was conscious too of getting back before sundown. They still had plenty of time, but that didn't make her feel any easier. After discovering the bone earlier, there was a possibility they were looking for ghosts. What if Tobias, Jane, and Ricardo were all dead? What if they were just wasting their time?

"Ma'am, I think I see something." Darius had stopped and was pointing to what appeared to be a huge pile of dung.

"Nice one, Darius," said Karl, "you just found the eighth wonder of the world. Dinosaur shit. Congratulations, you'll be a very rich man. Now perhaps we can get on with—"

"Hold up." Phoenix looked at it. The mound of dung had to be three feet across and was swarming with a thousand flies. There was almost no breeze up on the hillside, and the smell had been masked by two trees close by adorned with white flowers that gave off a musky smell.

"It's not the shit I'm interested in," said Darius. "Look there. It looks like there's something in it."

Phoenix spotted what Darius had seen and her hopes rose. "This could be another clue as to where we should be headed."

"Alex, fish that out," said Karl, finally seeing what it was that Darius had seen. There was a silver piece of metal sticking out of the center of the manure with what appeared to be blood on it. There was a scrap of cloth on it too, but it was covered in brown sticky gunk. They needed to see what it was and who it belonged to.

"Why me? Darius found it."

"Yeah and I outrank you," said Darius smiling, "so get on your hands and knees, and get digging through that shit."

Alex rolled up his sleeves and dropped to his knees. There was no way of reaching the metal without getting dirty. "Man, this smells so bad," he said as began to crawl into the dinosaur manure.

"Anyone bring a camera?" laughed Darius. "Man, this is priceless. Alex, you should be honored. We let you be the first man on the planet to crawl through dino shit and—"

A rumbling roar that rolled across the hill stopped the banter and Alex paused. The roar echoed across the jungle, and Phoenix looked across the treetops for its source. A couple of birds wheeled far away out to coast, but the island remained still.

A slight tremor ran up her leg and she looked at Alex. She knew what it meant. The vibrations running through the ground were a warning. "Hurry it up, Alex. Something big's coming."

CHAPTER 9

"Jesus, you smell bad. Get away from me, Alex. Toss that thing at my feet and find something to wipe yourself down with. Fuck."

Alex dropped the object he had plucked from the steaming pile of manure and removed his shirt. He found some dry leaves on the ground to wipe himself off with as the others examined what he'd found.

"Someone's going to have to clean it up so we can get a better look at it." Karl looked at Darius expectantly.

"I ain't touching it. You could catch anything."

Karl turned to Max. "Doctor? Care to do the honors?"

Max was already pulling on a pair of medical rubber gloves from his pack and bending down to the object. "Feces can contain enteric pathogens and bacteria that you really don't want to get into close contact with. Truly, you could catch something very nasty off this shit. Literally."

"Now he tells us," muttered Alex as he poured his bottled water over his arms and began scrubbing.

"Parasites and organisms live in the gut. Quite what would be present in a dinosaur's gut, I'm not sure. I guess we *are* all assuming this must be from our friend we ran into earlier?" Max looked at Phoenix and she nodded. Max wiped the object in his hands and turned it over. As it became cleaner, he was surprised to find it was a tablet. "Pass me one of those sterile wipes, will you? They're in the side pocket of my pack."

Karl grabbed them and handed them carefully to the doctor. Max rubbed the tablet clean as best he could and then handed it to Phoenix. Max stood up and discarded his gloves. "That's a Nexus

10X. They were issued to all our employees. I have one myself." Max sighed. "It has to belong to—"

"Another dead end." Phoenix passed it to Darius. "Don't suppose you can work your magic and see if there's any life in this?"

"I'll go take a look." Darius took the tablet from Phoenix. "Looks intact. The screen's not even broken. I'll try to power it up."

"You know, I hate to say it," said Karl ruefully, "but if that was in the dinosaur's shit, it's reasonable to assume it ate it. And unless it has a taste for electronics, then it's also reasonable to assume it ate whoever had it on them."

"I don't want to know," said Alex as he pulled his shirt back on. "Just tell me I didn't crawl through shit and that Justin didn't get nailed for nothing. Tell me some good news."

"It doesn't look good, does it?" said Phoenix rhetorically. Karl answered her with his eyes. "We press on. Another few minutes and we'll get a really good view of the island. We need to try to get a picture of what happened here. We don't know for certain that they are dead."

"As good as." Karl looked down the hillside to the jungle. "We barely made it out alive and we're armed soldiers. What hope would you give three unarmed civilians?"

"We can't give up now," said Max. "I can't leave not knowing for sure. What if they *are* alive? What if we gave up now and left them behind? We're so close. I know we are. We're so close to where we need to be."

"He's right." Phoenix looked out at the ocean. This operation wasn't over until they knew for sure. They had to find concrete evidence. Her hopes of finding anyone alive had faded considerably since leaving the jungle. "We'll get a little higher so that we can see some of the coves and beaches around the island. They may be stuck or hiding out. We need to cover every angle; check out every possibility until we are one hundred percent." Phoenix helped Max to his feet. "We're *not* leaving until we know."

Max picked up his pack. "I know how it looks. But I can't go back empty-handed. My bosses will want to know what happened."

"Um, I've got something here. Something big."

All eyes turned to Darius. He looked up from the tablet, his eyes wide. "It works. There's a video on here. It's pretty amazing."

"What is it?" Phoenix stood next to Darius as the others crowded around. "What did you find?"

"It actually works well. Don't ask me how. This thing has probably been places you wouldn't want to dream about. Right, Alex?"

"Fuck you." Alex punched Darius on the shoulder.

"Anyway," said Darius ignoring him, "the thing works." Darius swept his fingers across the touchscreen. "There's a bunch of files that I don't understand. Most of them seem to be about the probe they were looking for. Boring. But there was this weird-looking file on the desktop. I mean, it stood out because there's nothing else on here apart from stuff about rock samples, mission data, and Space54. So, I clicked on it."

"And?" Phoenix looked nervously over her shoulder. The island was quiet and she hadn't felt another rumble. The ground was still and it was unnerving. She knew that should be glad but somehow it was unsettling. "I assume you looked at it."

"What's on it?" asked Karl.

"Are they alive?" asked Max hopefully.

"See for yourself." Darius clicked open the video file and hit play. "There's no sound. Just watch."

Phoenix looked as the screen suddenly filled with something blurry and pink. The picture was shaking and then the pink blurriness faded as the camera panned out. It was a woman, a very pretty but scared-looking woman. She had blonde hair and a deep cut above one eye. Dirt was streaked down her face and she was looking directly at the camera.

"Jane! That's her, that's Jane," exclaimed Max. "She's alive."

Phoenix watched as the woman talked to the camera. Her mouth was moving, and it was apparent she was talking right into the lens, yet there was no audio.

"I think that the audio is corrupted," said Justin. "After what it's been through, we're lucky it works at all. I can try to look at that later."

Phoenix watched the young woman talk to the camera and then abruptly stop. She looked around and moved the camera slowly to the side, revealing the dense jungle. Phoenix recognized it as the one they had just been through. It was unmistakable.

"It's dated yesterday," said Justin. "This was recorded around twenty-six hours ago."

As Phoenix watched the camera pan around the jungle, she saw movement behind some of the trees. The camera stopped and panned out some more. A shaking slender arm appeared in the shot pointing at the jungle, and Phoenix wondered what the woman, Jane, was doing. She was probably providing a commentary, and it was frustrating not being able to hear her. She could be telling them where to find her, and yet all Phoenix could see was the thick jungle.

"This doesn't tell us anything," snapped Karl, rubbing the back of his head. "Turn it off, Justin. We should get moving before we're cooked to death."

"Wait a second."

Phoenix watched the screen as Jane's arm disappeared behind the camera. A dinosaur walked slowly through the jungle, moving between the trees. It looked like the one they had encountered earlier. Phoenix had seen it up close and knew it was the same one. She saw the blue eyes, the way it moved and the way it looked. The video jerked for a moment as Jane got to her feet and then her face filled the screen again. Tears were rolling down her face now in a flood, and Phoenix didn't need to be able to lip-read to know what she was saying.

'*Help me. Help me.*'

As the camera left Jane and pointed back at the jungle, the screen was suddenly filled with the dinosaur. It was barely ten feet away and looking right at it.

"Jesus. I don't think I want to see the rest," said Alex. "Tell me when it's over. I never did like horror films."

"Pussy," snorted Darius.

Phoenix put her hands over her mouth. She wanted to scream and tell Jane to run, to tell her to drop the camera and just run as fast as she could. But whatever happened was in the past. Seeing the dinosaur's face up close like that made her remember just what she had gone through. She had experienced the sheer power of the beast up close, and it looked as if Jane had too. Suddenly, the dinosaur attacked, rushing forward to the camera. The picture turned upside down, flashes of the green jungle and the dinosaur's blue eyes blurring into one. The video froze as Jane's face came into view one last time, the terror in her eyes making shivers run down Phoenix's spine. Just one of Jane's eyes was visible, and the dinosaur's jaws were right behind her. Phoenix felt sick as she looked at it. The video was frozen, her fear etched into a permanent record.

"That's it. There's no more. I think we can all guess what happened next." Justin turned the video off. "Probably good that it ends there," he said quietly.

Karl exhaled loudly. "Squad Leader. I think it's time we called it."

Phoenix didn't respond. She looked at Max. "What do you think?"

"Me?" The doctor rubbed the tears filling his eyes and swallowed nervously. "I don't know what to think anymore. I can't believe it. They came here to retrieve the samples from the crashed probe and they ended up in fucking Jurassic Park. What do I think? I think this is crazy."

"Hear, hear," said Alex. "This is crazy. Crazy that we're still standing here when we know that they're all dead."

"Do we?" Phoenix looked at Karl. Her heart was pounding in her chest. The video had been like a re-run of the attack on her and brought back all the fear she had felt. "You think she's dead? Jane's dead, right?"

"You saw the video. We pulled the tablet she filmed it on out of the dinosaur's shit. I'm sorry for the girl, but she didn't make it."

Phoenix nodded. "Of course. And what about me?"

"What about you?"

"I was as close to that monster as Jane was. It had me. So I must be dead too, right? There's no possible way that anyone could survive being attacked by that thing."

Karl rubbed his dry lips nervously. "Well, obviously you made it, but—"

"But nothing, Squad Leader. I made it. *And so did she*. That girl is on this island somewhere and we're going to find her."

"Sure we'll find her," interjected Darius. "She's about six feet behind you where we found this tablet. Right, Karl?"

"When was that video shot, Darius? Yesterday? So, we already know she made it for at least a day on the island. If she survived that long, then perhaps she had a hiding place, somewhere the dinosaur wouldn't or couldn't go."

"What about Ricardo and Tobias?" asked Karl. "They weren't on the video. And Jane was filming it herself which suggests they weren't with her."

"I'll worry about them when there's something to worry about. Maybe they made it, maybe they didn't. The only way we're going to get any answers is to scour this island for Jane. Right now, our efforts are going to be on finding that girl. We still have several hours of daylight so let's use them."

"Let's go," said Max. He began to trudge up the hill. "I want to hurry this up and find Jane."

"Okay, you heard the staff sergeant, let's rock and roll." Karl watched as Darius shoved the tablet in his pack. "Get moving, soldier." Darius and Alex began to follow Max.

"There's only so much they're prepared to do, you know," said Karl as he joined Phoenix. "They'll follow you into battle without question, but this is beginning to feel like we've been sent to look for a needle in a haystack."

"And you think the needle is dead. I get it, Karl, but what if Max is right?" Phoenix looked at Karl as they began to ascend the hill. "What if we left this island and she was still alive? Can you live with that? No matter how slim the chance that she's still alive, can you really leave?"

Karl looked up into the sun. "We'll give her as long as we can. But we're not missing that boat. I'll give Jane every inch of daylight I can, but once that sun goes down, we're gone."

"Deal."

As the sun beat down, they trudged onward and upward. The trees grew shorter and less frequent. The ground was hard and there was less soil for plant-life to grow in. The rocks became larger, and after a short while, they reached a plateau. The top of the peak was still some way up, but there was no need to go on. From where they had stopped, they had a view across almost the whole island.

"Darius, Alex, have some water and tell me what you see." Phoenix looked at where they had come from. The gentle hillside had been manageable, but if they continued any further, they would struggle in the heat of the day. The ascent got much steeper and there seemed little to gain from continuing. "Look for anything at all."

"I'm going to check out the other side of this plateau," said Karl. "If I've got my bearings right, then there will be a sheer drop to the ocean. I'll check it out and make sure our targets didn't go diving in the wrong place. Back in five."

Phoenix nodded as Karl scuttled away. "See anything?" she asked Max. He was staring out at the jungle, sweat visibly pouring down his red cheeks.

"Maybe. Maybe not. The probe came down somewhere on the island, but its precise location was unknown. I thought our team might have headed up here too, but I don't think they made it this far."

"True." Phoenix looked wistfully out at the ocean. The thought occurred to her that if Jane got away from the dinosaur, she might have tried to get off the island. What if she had a makeshift raft or had even swum for it? Then there would be no body to retrieve. "I hope we find them, Max. I know it looks grim, but I've talked to Karl. We'll give it a shot."

"Sure."

Max grunted, indicating he was done with the conversation. Phoenix left him staring at the jungle. She approached Darius and Alex, and then scoured the edge of the island for any sign of life. If Jane had made it to one of the many beaches, she may have left a sign. Plenty of rubbish and plastic washed up on the beaches and could've been used to put something together. Phoenix hoped she might see a shelter or even Jane herself. But as she looked around, she realized that there was nothing of note. From halfway up the island's peak, she could see some of the coral surrounding the island and wondered why the local chief didn't open up the place for tourism. If they could take care of their dinosaur problem, the island would be a magnet for rich tourists. The diving would be sensational and the beauty of the place was undeniable. Still, there was that problem of the resident dinosaur.

"Well, that was a waste of time," said Karl as he came jogging back around a large rock. "I was right about the drop. Must be two hundred feet all the way down. There's some nasty-looking rocks to cushion the fall, but I couldn't see any sign of our three missing people."

"Figures," said Phoenix despondently. "Unless the dinosaur chased them off the top of the peak, then I didn't really expect to find them up here."

"Well, from the size of that dump it took back there, we know it must've been up here, and recently. We'll find them soon. Or at least what's left of them." Karl called over to the others. "Darius, Alex, you got anything?"

The two soldiers shook their heads.

"What about you, Doc, you—?" Karl looked around for Max but couldn't see him. "Say, Phoenix, what did you do with our doctor?"

"He's right over there. He was looking over the jungle." Phoenix made her way back to where she had last seen the doctor. "Max?"

She took a few steps down the hill and called out again. "Max, where are you?" Silence greeted her and she looked at Karl. "Don't tell me he's wandered off on his own."

"Maybe he found something?" Karl didn't think it was likely. The doctor didn't strike him as being particularly brave or adventurous. If he had found something, then surely he would've spoken up.

"Could be he just went to take a leak," suggested Darius.

"You even thought about doing a piss since you got here?" asked Alex. "It's hotter than a hooker's asshole."

"Okay, boys, don't get started," said Phoenix, trying to get the image out of her mind.

"Max!" Karl shouted and then put two fingers to his lips. He let out a whistle that drifted over the whole jungle.

Nothing. Even the ocean's waves were silent, lost on the wind. The jungle remained quiet.

"Fuck, we're going to have to look for him," said Phoenix with her hands on her hips.

"Let's go," said Darius, picking up his pack. "We may as well head down anyway. We're not going to find anyone up here."

Phoenix kicked a rock in frustration. Not only had they not found who they had come here for, but they had managed to lose one of the unit and the doctor. "Max?" she called out, cupping her hands together. "Max, answer me!"

The thunderous roar that answered Phoenix made her bones shake. It was the monster again, only this time the sound was much closer. It didn't come from the jungle but the hilltop, seemingly close by. It went on for several seconds, and then the rock that she had kicked a moment earlier shifted. It jumped a fraction of an inch and Phoenix turned to Karl.

"Fuck," he whispered. "Darius, Alex, get your shit, we're leaving."

"I thought we'd lost it," said Phoenix as she raced to Darius. "I was hoping we'd scared that bastard off."

"Maybe it can smell us. In this heat, my deodorant is working overtime."

"Come on, pick up the pace," ordered Karl as he began to make his way down the hill. Alex was right behind him. "I don't like being out in the open like this. We need to find cover."

The ground shook again, causing several loose rocks to tumble past them. A thin tree next to Phoenix shuddered and she knew the dinosaur was close.

She heard running, panting, and then Max appeared. He was charging up the hill, his face redder than a clown's nose.

"Get back, get away," he shouted as he ran toward them waving his hands above his head. "It's coming!"

CHAPTER 10

The doctor ran past Phoenix with surprising speed for his age. She didn't need to ask him what he was running from. The fear on his face and the roar of the dinosaur spurred her into action and she turned on her heels.

"Go!" Phoenix gave Darius a push and he began to run after the doctor. "Karl, Alex, hurry it up."

They quickly reached a point where it appeared to be safe to stop. Phoenix looked back to see Karl and Alex a little way behind her. Over the sparse trees and crumbling rocks, she saw it. The dinosaur was charging up the hill, its powerful legs making light work of the incline. It smashed through the bushes and trees with ease, making a beeline for them.

"Darius, do your thing," she ordered, wishing she had a weapon. She watched him drop to one knee and pull out his gun.

"With pleasure." Darius fired a round over Karl's head. The bullets bounced off the dinosaur's skull. It didn't slow.

"Go again," ordered Phoenix.

As Darius fired again, she looked for Max. He was just above her, cowering behind a large boulder. She had a few questions for him, not least where he had disappeared to and why he had brought that thing back with him. Maybe it was an unlucky coincidence, but his timing was terrible. The only way off the island was down the hill and back through the jungle, and now their access was blocked. She knew they didn't have enough firepower to kill it.

"Max, wait there." Phoenix saw Karl and Alex split up. Alex sprinted to the left and Karl kept straight on up the hill. The dinosaur's large eyes quickly took in its prey and then it kept going, gaining quickly on Karl.

"Darius, keep shooting, we might get lucky and scare it off. Watch your back."

Phoenix charged up the hill to the doctor and skidded to halt next to him, churning up a cloud of dust. After the tropical jungle, the land was dry and unwelcoming. The sun made everything hot to touch, and she winced as she put her hands on a large boulder. A small lizard, no bigger than her little finger, skittered across to the slim shade of a nearby tree.

"Help me." Phoenix began to push on the boulder and the doctor joined her. "It's all I can think of."

The boulder at first refused to budge, but as they kept pushing on it, gravity took over. It slipped a couple of inches and then began to roll. It would flatten any of the fragile trees in its path, but Phoenix wasn't so sure about the dinosaur. It at least would surely give it a nudge in the wrong direction.

"Darius, Karl, watch out!" Phoenix watched as the boulder picked up speed and began to bounce down the hillside right toward the dinosaur. Darius crouched down as it went past him, colliding with other boulders and smashing through the brittle trunks of the bushes and short trees. Phoenix saw Karl duck to his right, toward the edge of the plateau, dodging the rocks that were tumbling downhill.

The dinosaur reared up as the boulder approached. The creature let out another shuddering roar and then lowered its head. The boulder smashed into it and broke in half. Phoenix watched in amazement as the boulder was destroyed.

"Jesus, did you see that?" asked Max. "That thing is tough."

Phoenix scoured the hill for Karl and Alex. "You sound impressed."

"Aren't you?"

"I don't have time to be impressed when I'm trying to save my unit." Phoenix scrambled to her feet. The dinosaur appeared to be dazed. It was tough but not impervious to pain. Evidently, the boulder had done enough to buy them a few seconds. Phoenix looked around for another way down the hill. To the left was the sheer drop that Karl had spoken of. There was little point in jumping hundreds of feet onto the rocks down below. Around to the west was their only chance. She didn't know what sort of terrain they faced, but it was the only viable choice.

"Let's move out. Follow me." Phoenix grabbed the doctor's arm and began to run. She saw Darius, Karl, and Alex all begin to follow her. They all had their guns out now and were firing at the dinosaur. It took a few steps back, and for a moment, she thought that it might back off. Maybe it had realized they could hurt it, that this was a fight it wasn't going to win easily. The dinosaur snorted and then lowered its head and began to run at them.

"Shit," muttered Max.

The hillside levelled out, and Phoenix found she was running through open land. The trees and plants abruptly stopped and she plunged into shadow. The island's volcanic peak obliterated the sun and little appeared to grow here. The flat ground did not last long and the incline became almost impossible to navigate. The surface of the hill was slippery with shale and loose stones, and running was out of the question. She paused and the doctor stopped a few feet ahead of her.

"Why are you stopping?" he asked. "Come on."

Phoenix glared at him. "I'm not going *anywhere* without my unit." Her lungs hurt from running through the heat and her shoulder ached. Her jaw felt like it had taken a beating from a heavyweight boxer, and now her feet were struggling to gain traction in the loose dirt and rocks. "And neither are you. Wait there."

Phoenix looked back. She shivered as the cool air on this side of the hill began to quickly cool her down. Looking at where they had come from, she saw Darius, rapidly followed by Karl and Alex. As soon as they reached the slippery ground, they slowed down too. They had escaped the hillside only to emerge in a much more difficult area. The incline and shallow, loose dirt threatened to trip them up every second.

"Come to me," she urged. "This way."

The dinosaur appeared behind them, and as it took a step into the shadows, it hesitated. Phoenix smiled. It knew this island, this ground, and it knew when to stop. Surely it wouldn't risk following them here? It had to know it wasn't safe. She could barely stand up herself and the weight of the dinosaur would surely be too much.

"Holy hell," said Darius breathlessly as he reached Phoenix. He leant over and put his hands on his knees. "I need to work out more."

Phoenix snatched Darius' weapon off him and aimed at the dinosaur. She looked at its blue eyes and tried to pick one out. If she could blind it, then they would really gain the upper hand. She squeezed the trigger and the barrel clicked empty.

"Sorry, I'm all out," said Darius. "I unloaded everything I had back there. Guess we'll have to keep our fingers crossed and say our prayers."

Phoenix watched the dinosaur take another step onto the hillside, hesitate, and then being to move forward. It was still coming, apparently unafraid of the dangerous slope they were on. She couldn't believe it. She looked around for something else she could use to ward it off, but there was nothing. Scaling the upper peak was impossible and the only way down was to try and use the slippery ground until they reached the jungle. It would be nearly impossible to stay on their feet. They had to go on. If they fell, there would be nothing to stop them continuing down to whatever awaited them at the bottom. The hillside just dropped fifty feet or so and then disappeared. The jungle lay somewhere beyond it, and then the crystal-clear ocean, but Phoenix could not see what was in between. She suspected it would be a painful fall and very likely an even worse landing. The harsh landscape suggested this was not a place for humans. This was the dinosaur's land. Maybe that was why it was still coming, despite the inherent danger. It wasn't going to back off until they had left. They were the enemy here, *they* were the invaders; Phoenix knew they had to leave.

"This way," said Phoenix. Karl reached her just as she began to make her way to the doctor. "We have to keep going, outrun that thing. It's not going to stop."

"Outrun it?" Karl dropped to his knees and opened his pack. He pulled out a grenade. "No chance. We have to take it out while we can."

"You can't use that here," said Phoenix through gritted teeth. "You'll bring the whole side of the mountain down on us. It's too dangerous."

"We'll see. I'm keeping it handy. Just in case." Karl jumped to his feet. "I think we—"

"Oh no, Alex. No!"

Phoenix heard Darius call out and looked over to Alex. The soldier had tripped and was scrambling to get to his feet. There was nothing solid to get hold of, and every time he stood up, he fell back down. The dinosaur was gaining on him rapidly.

"We have to do something." Darius looked at Phoenix. "Please. We have to do *something*."

Phoenix felt helpless. Their guns were useless, and they were reduced to their wits and fists. It wasn't a fair fight. That was why they had to outrun it. They *had* to outsmart it.

"Karl? How good an aim are you?" Phoenix eyed up his grenade. "Can you really take it out from here?"

Karl shook his head. "Not without risking Alex too."

As Phoenix watched Alex get to his feet, she knew it was almost too late. The dinosaur was right on top of him. She grabbed the grenade from Karl's hand.

"Don't," growled Karl. "You can't be sure of not hitting him."

"Fuck it." Darius began to make his way back across the slope toward Alex. "I'll get him myself."

"Darius, get back here!"

"We're not leaving him behind," yelled Darius. "We might be out of bullets, but we're not out of balls."

"God damn it, he'll never make it." Karl snatched the grenade back off Phoenix. "Darius, Alex, get down. I'm tossing the grenade. I'll aim high. As soon as it goes, you get over here."

Karl pulled the pin and drew back his arm. Sweat dripped off his muscles.

"I thought you said it was too risky." Phoenix felt sick. She wanted to run after them too, to drag Darius and Alex back, but she knew there was no way she would make it. The dinosaur was barely twenty feet behind Alex and was gaining fast. Its weight if anything was actually helping it. Its huge feet crushed anything in its path, and even though Alex was bursting with energy and adrenalin, it wasn't going to be enough.

"No time for anything else." Karl threw the grenade as high and hard as he could. "Get down!" he yelled, and he pushed Phoenix behind him.

She caught sight of the doctor's mouth agape as he cringed in disbelief. Karl pushed her down and then she felt the shattering explosion. The boom of the grenade exploding was quickly followed by the ear-piercing roar of the dinosaur. Phoenix felt as if she was back in Mosul, shrapnel and bullets flying past her head. She heard the shouts of men in agony and the familiar feeling that she was going to die. Shards of volcanic rock showered over them like crumbling masonry. The sky spewed out splinters and shrapnel, sending it down, down, down, fast and as lethal as a sniper's bullets. Phoenix cradled her head, knowing that the soft military cap she wore and her short brown hair offered no protection. Razors rained down on her skin, raking across the tissue, leaving bloody cuts on her arms and hands. The searing heat from the fire warmed her back and then she felt Karl grab her.

"You okay?"

Phoenix rolled over and looked up at him. "Yeah. Yeah, I'm okay." She blinked. Dust ballooned above them and she heard more shouting.

"Get up," said Karl as he put a strong arm underneath her. "I think we just pissed it off."

Phoenix heard the mournful cry of the dinosaur as she struggled to pull herself up. The rocky ground felt like sludge. Her boots were sinking into the gravel, and it was only leaning on Karl that got her to her feet.

"Max, you all good?" she asked.

The doctor nodded, but his face was white. He looked as if he was in shock. He opened his mouth to speak, but no sound came out.

"Good," said Phoenix, not really caring what Max was feeling or thinking. He was the least of her worries.

As the dust cloud began to clear, Phoenix saw what damage the grenade had done. Darius was doubled over, coughing and spluttering as he made his way back to them. Alex too was retching as the dust cloud dissipated. Evidently, Karl had thrown it far enough to avoid them and they were seemingly uninjured. Several rocks were tumbling down the hillside and the ground was trembling. It felt as if a volcano had been awakened. Phoenix saw the dinosaur struggling to maintain its balance behind Alex. The grenade appeared to have exploded close to it as blood poured down the monster's left flank. The monster was bellowing with rage, pain, and frustration. A large rock the size of a minivan flew past Alex, narrowly missing him.

"Come on, come on," urged Phoenix. As she held onto Karl, she felt her feet begin to slide downward. "We need to get away from here."

"As soon as we've got our boys, I'll be right with you." Karl gritted his teeth. "This hillside is getting worse every second. I don't know if—"

A dull boom reached their ears, sounding almost as if a submarine had hit the ocean floor. Yet it came from under their feet, under the hillside. The loose rocks around Phoenix's feet began to move and the land began to subside. A waspy tree covered in butterflies began to tilt toward the horizon and the swarm of insects rose off it into the blue sky. She grabbed hold of Karl, but he was falling too.

"Alex, we gotta go now!" she shouted. The dinosaur was falling too, unable to sustain its balance anymore. It was like a huge skyscraper turning and twisting as it fell. The grey cloud thrown up by the devastated rock surrounding it reminded Phoenix of Iraq and the war-torn towns she had been through. The monster bellowed mournfully as it toppled—right over Alex.

"Help, I can't—"

Phoenix saw the fear etched on the young soldier's face. His feet were barely clinging to the surface of the hill, his forlorn face shrouded in the shadow of the beast.

Alex reached out an arm and Phoenix stretched her hand to him. He was too far away and she was moving away from him as the hill collapsed. Phoenix saw the dinosaur fall on top of Alex. He was submerged beneath its hide and then she lost everything. The hillside became a tumultuous river of rocks and dirt. She toppled over along with Karl and began to tumble down the hill, every bone in her body rattling and bouncing off the rocks hurtling around her. She heard the doctor cry out and caught a glimpse of his white hair as he flew past her. She tried to keep in contact with Karl, but he fell away from her. Her fingers reached for him, but he slipped from her and she just brushed his arm as he cartwheeled above her. Silhouetted up against the blue sky, she noticed he didn't look afraid, just angry and frustrated. A large boulder with cold green algae on its underbelly struck her in the center of her back and she saw stars. Blackness took over her vision then and she felt her face strike the moving ground. There was nothing to slow her fall, and the world began to spin around and around. The blue sky, the grey dirt and rocks, Karl's khaki uniform, and her own blood mingled to create a canvas of chaos. Her hands reached for something solid to hold onto, but she either grasped thin air or a handful of loose dirt that had no more power to stop tumbling down the hill than she had.

"Phoenix!"

She felt something warm strike her body and then she suddenly came to a stop. It was like hitting a brick wall and the impact knocked the breath out of her. She had come to rest against a large Psydrax Odorata, its roots slowly being torn up by the torrent of rocks striking it.

"*Phoenix.*"

The voice was fainter this time. Her head felt like she'd only just awoken from a vodka-coma, and the voice was barely strong enough to snap her into full consciousness. She rubbed her eyes, amazed that it was over, amazed that they hadn't fallen over a precipice large enough to break all the bones in their bodies. The landslide had stopped. The warm object that had landed next to her began to move and she reached a hand out.

"Karl? Is it over?"

Blood trickled over her lips, and Phoenix wiped it away as she gently moved her hand over the body. As the fizzing stars disappeared from her eyes, she realized that it wasn't Karl. The body was slimmer, and even though it was one of her unit, she knew it couldn't be him. The tree she was leaning on jerked spasmodically and she gripped the leg of the man beside her.

"Ph—"

The body moved and she saw Darius looking at her through a haze of blood. It ran down his face from the numerous abrasions to his head. One of his arms had been twisted around and was undoubtedly broken. She felt more blood beneath the pant leg that she had hold of.

"Darius, what happened to the others?" Phoenix looked around, but the world had turned gray. There was no horizon, no ocean, no jungle, just an interminable endless gray of dirt and dust. She was half-buried in the loose stones and her body ached. Then Phoenix felt the ground beneath her begin to go again and she looked at Darius for answers that he didn't have. "What happ—?"

The small tree gave away, its roots tearing up out of the ground. It sounded to Phoenix much like a hurricane ripping the roof off a barn. She had survived enough storms to know the sound when she heard it, and she knew there would be casualties from this. This was real. The hillside had collapsed in on itself, and they were all going to be hurting when it finally came to a halt. Phoenix was flung backwards and she lost Darius in the ensuing tumult. She continued falling, swept away in the swollen river of rocks. There was a roar echoing across the sky and she knew it wasn't the island. It was the dinosaur. The monster wasn't dead but falling with them, unable to stop. She felt something sharp bang against her head and open up a deep cut across her chin. Another rock bounced off her right thigh and her hands raked across the ground. It felt like it was going on forever. In trying to escape the dinosaur, they had only succeeded in making things worse. Is that what had happened to Tobias, Jane, and Ricardo? Had they encountered this thing too? The avalanche continued taking her down, and she had no idea when it would stop, or where.

Phoenix tried to scream, to plead for it to stop, to beg for it to be over for her and her unit, but when she opened her mouth, dirt rushed in. It was like being covered in snow, just as suffocating and encompassing, and she knew all she could do was ride it out and pray. Her sisters were thousands of miles away, probably ordering a latté to go with their blueberry muffin while considering how much more they could add onto their mortgage. The bosses at Space54 were safely in their air-conditioned offices already planning the next mission into space, unaware of how many people they had condemned to death by sending them to this island. And Freddy might be waiting on his boat, or he might already be back home with his family, forgetting all about the stupid soldiers he had brought to the island of death. Slowly but surely, they were being butchered. They had underestimated the island big-time.

Phoenix became aware that suddenly her feet and arms and legs were no longer scrambling around in the dirt but free. She felt cool air embrace her and she found herself looking up at the sky. She felt like she was flying, free from the burden of responsibility for this mess, free from the dinosaur's grasp on her unit and free from the island. God, how she hated it now. She hated that she had misjudged it so badly. She hated how she had to be the tomboy out of her three sisters. She hated how she knew she was going to die having missed out on so much life. Why couldn't she be the one sitting in a coffee shop with a husband instead of bickering with Karl? Why couldn't she be the one wearing Levi 501s and driving home for Christmas instead of sweating in a tent in the middle of a barren desert?

A man screamed next to her and she saw Max fly past her. It dawned on her that they had reached the edge of the cliff. The hillside didn't slope down forever until it reached the jungle. The hill was as deadly as everything else on this forsaken, forgotten island. The blue sky above her was no comfort. It didn't matter if she died in paradise or a ditch with her legs blown off: dead was dead.

Phoenix yelled in fear and then saw two men flying above her. Several trees were tumbling from the hillside amid a multitude of rocks which varied in size from golf balls to a 4WD. Then she saw the dinosaur. Its arms and legs were flailing uselessly, its monstrous body obliterating the sun. It looked like an airship slowly deflating, unable to maintain its place in the sky. She saw sunlight shine off its teeth as it bellowed and snapped its jaws. One of her men, too far away for her to be able to recognize, was right next to it. The dinosaur's teeth were snapping at him, as if it wanted to try and eat them even while falling to its own death. Phoenix opened her mouth to scream and then lost her breath as icy cold water wrapped around her.

She plunged abruptly into darkness, the sunlight and sky a distant blurry vision above the surface of the water. Water raced into her mouth as she tried to focus on staying alive. She guessed she had sunk fifteen feet or more, yet she did not hit the bottom of whatever they had landed in. She had been waiting to hit rocks, but the water had broken her fall, and even though she was showering underneath a hillside collapsing on top of her, she knew there was still a chance. Phoenix kicked upwards, her lungs burning with the precious little air she had in her. She tried to swim up to the surface, but there was a current pulling her the other way. The surface was getting closer, but it took all her energy to get there and fight the current that was trying to pull her down. Finally, her head broke the surface of the water and she quickly sucked in huge mouthfuls of air. She heaved and heard splashing noises around her. She heard someone call out for help, but couldn't identify who it was. She tried to tread water, but she was drifting downstream, and she looked up to see if there were some overhanging vines she could grab hold of. When she looked up at where they had come from, she felt all hope in her die. The dinosaur was falling, fast, and it was coming right for her. Its jaws were snapping loudly, eagerly, searching for something to bite. She waited for the impact, her shoulders sagging as her legs strained to keep her head above water. She had been so close. She had tasted freedom and life for a moment then. Even when the water had engulfed her, she thought there was still a way to get off the island and home alive. As the dinosaur angrily rushed toward her, she knew the only way home was in a body bag. And as the ice-cold water tugged at her feet, she let her body go. She let go of memories of her sisters, of any chance she might have of seeing Karl or home again, and closed her eyes. It was over.

CHAPTER 11

Its eyes darted cautiously around the upper tree branches and the bird risked a mating call. The island was its home although recently things had changed. The bird had seen unusual creatures descend upon the island, yet it didn't bother with them. It ruffled its feathers and chirruped. It made no matter. The monster never bothered with it. The bird had seen the creatures falling from the sky. It wondered why they didn't fly away to safety, but only for a moment. It was preoccupied with finding a mate. Its dark green feathers hid it well in the upper branches of the trees, and it had a full belly after gorging on bugs disturbed from their nests and homes by the strange creatures. It darted away from the invaders and left them alone. The island would take care of them; it always did. The bird whistled and heard a faint reply. It was time to move on.

Phoenix coughed up a salty mixture of blood and water, and reached a hand up onto a slimy rock. It was damp, but held firm, and she pulled her aching body out of the lagoon. She hauled herself up the stony bank out of the water and rolled over onto a flat rock. A shaft of sunlight filtered through the protective trees and its warmth on her cheek felt good. The spot of sunlight was no larger than a dollar coin, but she would take it. She coughed up again, not caring that the bloody saliva was rolling down her cheek. She didn't care what she looked like. She was just grateful and amazed in equal measure that she was still breathing. Phoenix looked up at the sky and the green trees waving gently at her. A tiny bird with dark green plumage flitted between the branches, seemingly looking for food. The trees remained motionless, oblivious to what had just happened. It was just another day for them, just another twenty-four hours of soaking up the life-giving rays of the sun. Phoenix sat up reluctantly and immediately her head swam. She placed both of her palms flat on the rock and waiting for the head rush to subside. Quite how or why she was still alive, she didn't know. The dinosaur had impacted upon the water right above her. It had driven her under water, and somewhere in that icy cold maelstrom the dinosaur had been right alongside her. Somehow, she had avoided becoming lunch for it for a second time. She was aware of being swept along under water, over and over as if she were inside a giant washing machine until she had blacked out. She had come around a minute ago, on the banks of the lagoon. She looked around and her suspicions were realized. It was the same one, the same damn lagoon: they were back where they had started.

Phoenix slowly got to her feet. She knew that any sudden movements would likely bring on another dizzy spell, so she moved very slowly. When she was finally upright, she looked for the rest of her unit. They had ended up in the river that fed it and had now devoured half of the hill. The waterfall that had poured into the lagoon earlier was now just a trickle. A huge dam had formed above it, made mostly out of boulders and trees. Yet atop it all was the dinosaur. Phoenix tensed up when she saw it. Its blue eyes were looking right at her, and its two arms were perched above the waterfall as if it was about to climb right over it and down to her. She took a step back and waited for it to roar or to attack. She waited a full ten seconds, counting slowly and silently in her head, before doubt began to gnaw at her belly. She let the pain in her body wake her up some more and she continued to stare at the creature. Its blue eyes were still looking at her, but it wasn't moving. As she began to skirt around the edge of the lagoon, she saw that it wasn't getting up or doing anything. It wasn't even breathing. The closer she got, the more she knew for certain that it was dead. A smile escaped the corner of her mouth. It flitted there momentarily before pain extinguished it. The titan's blood was gushing over the waterfall into the lagoon, and the sight of all that blood-red water reminded Phoenix that her unit was still missing. Some of that blood could be theirs. Still, the thought refused to leave her. They had done it. They had killed it.

Phoenix bent over and laughed. Her abdomen was racked with pain as she laughed, but she couldn't stop it. Her body shook and her laughter turned into a coughing fit. It was absurd. They had just killed a *dinosaur*. She looked up and saw its dead eyes looking at her, and Phoenix laughed again. Who was she kidding? She wasn't cut out for a suburban life like her sisters. She wouldn't have wanted to miss out on this. She didn't know how the day was going to end, but when she closed her eyes, she at least could say she had looked into the eyes of death and fought back.

"Oh, shit the bed, this is unreal." Phoenix spat and straightened her back. The hot sun formed droplets of sweat and the salty water stung her wounds. She was mildly surprised that nothing was broken, but knew her unit were almost certainly not going to be as fortunate. She still hadn't seen any of them since waking.

"Good afternoon campers, anyone here?" Phoenix called out, her voice carrying across the water. The high-pitched squawk of a distant bird answered her over the gentle lapping over the water near her feet. Something rustled in the shrubs behind her and she turned around.

"Little help?"

Phoenix jumped, startled by the voice. She looked at the rocks around her and then finally spotted Karl, one arm outstretched and reaching up into the sky.

"Jesus." Phoenix raced to him, ignoring the pain that erupted in her right leg as she ran, and grabbed him with both hands. She pulled him to her, grateful to find somebody else alive.

"Okay, well that hurt." Karl exhaled and rubbed the back of his shaven head. "Like, a lot."

"How the hell did you get here?" asked Phoenix. She looked over him. It was miraculous that he was still in one piece. Lacerations and blood covered his body, and his shirt had been ripped to pieces, but he appeared to be in good health considering.

"Same as you, I guess." Karl looked at her and immediately tore off a scrap of cotton on the end of his shirt. He used it to dab at the cuts on Phoenix' head as they knelt at the edge of the crimson lagoon. He began to wipe away the blood and dirt that was smeared across her face. "I saw the beast come down on top of you. I thought you were history. The water took me over the edge of those rocks and I swam here. I felt kinda woozy, so I was just taking a minute to get my breath back. I think I blacked out for a while. It felt quite peaceful just lying there if I'm honest. I was hoping I'd dreamt it all."

"Me too." Phoenix winced as Karl drew the cotton across her chin. He cupped one hand around her face and examined her closely. "You're going to need stitches in that."

Phoenix shrugged. The weight of responsibility was hovering over her again. Stitches would have to wait. "I guess we should find the doctor and the others. I expect everyone is going to have a few cuts and bruises to attend to." She remembered Darius. She remembered how he looked. He was going to need more than a few stitches.

Karl kept his hand on her face and raised her eyes up to his. His brown eyes bore into hers. "We did the right thing. Whatever comes out of this, it isn't on us. If we'd stayed up there on that mountain, she would've killed us all. That bitch wasn't going to stop until it had taken a giant bite out of each and every one of us. It would've brought the hillside down anyway even if we hadn't. That grenade just gave us a chance."

Carrying the bodies of Sawyer and Travers out of Mosul, Phoenix thought she would never be in such a position again, and certainly not on this operation.

"I thought I was dead," said Phoenix quietly. She shivered, her damp clothes in the shadow of the tall trees making her feel cold despite the adrenalin and the incessant sunshine hiding above the canopy. The sweat on her body felt cold once she was out of direct sunlight.

"Well, I for one am glad you're not." Karl got to his feet and pulled Phoenix up. He grinned. "If you'd died, I'd have no one to bitch to. All right, Fifi, let's round up the others and get the hell out of dodge."

Phoenix took the scrap of cotton from him and dabbed at her bleeding chin. She had always felt a grudging respect for Karl but rarely seen his softer side. He had a teenage daughter back in Chicago, but he almost never spoke of her or his ex-wife. It was as if he had to keep up the image he had of a tough soldier and anything that might suggest he was human after all might impact upon his reputation. She could see how he filled the role well. He worked out all the time and his olive skin and muscles brought him a lot of attention. He never told her why he had broken up with his wife, never talked about why his brother had gone off the rails. It was better that way. Let him have his secrets. They worked well together, despite their differences. Even though he could be a royal pain in the ass, it was good to have him on her side. He pushed her, made her be better than she might otherwise be.

"Darius? Alex? Get your damn asses out here!" shouted Karl.

As they scanned the area for any sign of life, Phoenix and Karl couldn't help but smile at the sight of the dead dinosaur. They had gotten lucky. It was dead and its rotting carcass would take weeks to decompose.

"There," said Phoenix finally, pointing out movement on the far side of the lagoon. "Is that Alex?"

They raced around to the forlorn figure and found Alex struggling to his feet.

"Damn, feels like a truck hit me," said Alex, clutching his head.

"Looks like it, too," replied Phoenix. Alex was intact, though his face had already started to bruise and his left eye was sporting a nasty-looking cut under it.

"You'll do just fine, Private." Karl and Phoenix helped him up. "Any sign of the doc or Darius?"

Alex rolled his neck around his shoulders. "You mean before or after that fucking dinosaur landed on top of me?" He ran a hand over his closely shaved head. "Sorry, sorry. I know."

"*Did* you see them?" asked Phoenix, folding her arms. The jungle was around them again and that meant one thing: they could retrace their path back to the beach. Within an hour or two, they could be back on the beach waiting for Freddy to take them away from the island. The sooner they had Darius and Max back, they could get moving. "Can you remember anything at all?"

Alex leant down at the water's edge, cupped his hands, and splashed water over his head. "Not much after the explosion. I know that bitch took a hit," he said, looking over at the dead dinosaur. "But it didn't kill her. Must've been the fall that finally did it. I didn't see what happened to you or anyone else. All I know is that thing landed on me and then I was falling with it. Christ, I thought it was going to eat me as we were falling, you know? If we hadn't landed in the water, we'd be toast. No doubt that if you hadn't tossed the grenade when you did, I would've been dead meat. That thing would've eaten me whole."

"Yeah, but a scrawny thing like you would've only been like an appetizer," said Karl. "Änd another thing, you still smell like shit, Alex. You might want to scrub up."

Phoenix looked again at the dinosaur. It was hard to believe, but it was truly dead. The bulk of its body had come to rest behind the waterfall along with half of the hillside. The water running off the mountain was building up, unable to get past the unorthodox damn apart from in a slow trickle. They had discovered a prehistoric monster, something that human eyes had never seen apart from in books and Spielberg movies, and then they had killed it. Would they be judged on that? Would the world understand?

"Ma'am, does your leg hurt?" asked Alex as he splashed water over his face.

"Hm? Why?" It did hurt, but she had forgotten about it. So much of her body hurt that all her pain had bundled itself up into a neat little ball which she had stowed away for the future. She had more to contend with, like finding the rest of her unit and explaining how they had killed the only living dinosaur in the world, than complaining about a few cuts and bruises.

"Well, for one thing, you've got a giant fucking tooth stick out of it," replied Alex.

Phoenix looked down and saw it. Jutting out of her right thigh was what looked like a bone. It was yellow and jagged down one side, and bizarrely yet undeniably a tooth. The sharp end was only a couple of inches away from her groin.

"Shit, so that's what that is." Phoenix went to pull it out, but Karl stopped her.

"No, not yet. If you pull it out now, you might hit an artery. We need to find a compress or bandage to stop any bleeding. Wait until we find the doctor. Hopefully Max might still have his kit with him. He still had it on his back when the hill collapsed."

"Damn it, my bag," said Alex, looking around. "I lost it."

"Don't sweat it, soldier." Phoenix knew they were out of everything. They had no weapons, no food or water, and no radio. "We all lost our packs. Just be thankful you're still alive. We'll be lucky if any of our gear turns up. I think it's buried under that monster."

"Okay, we need to find Darius and Max. Then we're out of here," said Karl, looking at Phoenix. "*Don't* tell me we're still going to try to find those three saps from Space54. I think it's safe to say they're dead."

"We're leaving," agreed Phoenix. "Just as soon as we find—"

As she looked out across the lagoon toward the dinosaur, she caught sight of something out of place. She put her hands above her eyes and squinted. Beneath the dinosaur was an arm, lying across a rock, and the body it was attached to lay out of sight.

"Damn it, I think that's Darius," she said. It could have been the doctor, but something about the complexion of the skin made her think otherwise. "We have to get up there. Alex, stay here," ordered Phoenix. "Look around for the doctor. Karl and I will go check on Darius."

"But—"

"*Wait.*" Phoenix began to scamper after Karl who was already clambering over scorching hot boulders to the top of the waterfall. "And find the doctor!"

Phoenix followed Karl's path, knowing he had a natural ability that would see him skip over the rocks in twice the time it took her to. He used some vines as makeshift ropes and was soon around the edge of the lagoon, gaining height as he rapidly climbed around the dwindling falls. Karl was quicker than her and nimble on his feet despite his size. When she caught up with him, he was already standing atop the dinosaur as if he had conquered Everest. She could imagine him planting a flag in the beast's hide and claiming it for America.

"Down here," yelled Karl.

He disappeared as he slid down the belly of the dinosaur and Phoenix raced after him. Every step she took caused the tooth in her leg to send shuddering pain through her body, but she just wanted to get Darius out of there. The monster smelt foul, as if it had already started to rot. As she climbed its carcass, she was even more amazed at its bulk. It was a true monster, an abomination that had no right to exist. She didn't feel even slightly bad for killing it. It had been it or them. It felt surreal as she reached its apex. She could see back down the river that fed the waterfall and down to the edge of the lagoon. She peered up at the hill, but there was just a giant dust cloud where it had been. It hung suspended over the island like a protective shield. She could also see the massive injury the grenade had caused to the dinosaur. Blood still oozed from its side where she could see its pink flesh and rubbery innards. As she scanned the monster, she noticed that its head was cocked to one side, not in line with its body. She surmised that in the fall it had broken its neck. Perhaps it had drowned. Whatever had killed it, she was just pleased it was over.

Phoenix slid down the beast's belly and found Karl down on his knees. The edge of the waterfall was close and the stink of the dinosaur was almost overwhelming. It was as if the burning sun was already making its body expand and rot in the heat, and she imagined how many scavengers it would take to strip the thing down to its bones.

"How is he?" Phoenix saw Darius lying on a rock next to the beast. The turgid water was flowing around him, lazily snaking its way between the flat rocks until it descended into the lagoon. One of Darius' legs was trapped under the dinosaur and one of his arms had been twisted into an unnatural position. His eyes were closed and Karl was holding his hand. Phoenix bent down next to them, unable to kneel because of the burgeoning pain in her leg. She looked at Karl and felt her heart flutter.

"He's gone."

Karl uttered the words in a monotone voice. There was no sympathy in those two words, and he kept his eyes on Darius when he spoke. He delivered Phoenix the bad news as if he were reading out the sports results.

"No," Phoenix whispered as she looked at Darius. She didn't want to accept it, didn't want to believe Karl, yet she knew it was the truth. Blood seeped from Darius' closed lips and his chest wasn't moving. The dinosaur had claimed one last victim before succumbing to death itself. She straightened up and sighed. She had lost two of her men on this island. The operation was not just over but a complete failure. Two men. She hadn't expected to lose anyone today. She had hoped she might be returning to base with three extra people, but she was going to have to explain how she had lost Justin and Darius.

Karl yanked the dog tags from Darius' neck, shoved them in his pocket, and stood up. "It's this island. This fucking island." He turned to look at Phoenix. "How could Freddy not know about this place? How could anyone not know about this?" Karl kicked the dead dinosaur, his boot striking its leathery hide with a solid thud.

"You don't know what you don't know. Why would anyone have reason to think there was anything dangerous on this island?" Phoenix looked at Karl. His deep brown eyes were angry. He felt responsible too, she could tell, but this was on her. "I should've pushed for more information. I thought this was going to be easy. I thought this was going to be simple."

"It's not you." Karl kicked the dinosaur again. "I'm sorry, I just... I've known Darius for years. It's hard to accept that he and Justin aren't coming back with us."

Phoenix looked up at the sky. She twisted her neck away from the sun, but the heat was incessant. She felt a fly crawl across her crown and slapped it away. Another landed on her cheek and she angrily brushed it away with her hand. Had they found the dinosaur already? "We have to get back to Alex. Maybe he found the doctor. We're leaving, Karl. It's over. Quite honestly, we're lucky that any of us are going home. Given the situation—" Phoenix shrugged.

"I know." Karl looked at her. "Okay, let's find the doc and get you seen to. Then we'll get off this damn island." He began to climb the beast, pulling himself up and over. "Let's go. I have to tell Alex."

Phoenix felt woozy. She put her hand to her throat. The skin was warm, and as she rubbed the back of her neck, she felt sweat run down her back. Karl had a way of switching off, of going into auto-pilot. He took all the emotion out of the situation; the only glimpse into his real thoughts was when he showed his anger. She wanted to cry for Darius but refused to. She had to get things back under control. Now that the dinosaur was dead, they could regroup, find the doctor, and find a way back to the beach. The heat was killing her though. It was even worse than on the Reagan. It was sapping her strength and she could feel her body wanting to give in. She wondered if she could jump back into the lagoon from here instead of following Karl. He was already halfway down, swinging across a large boulder on a vine, as if he were Tarzan.

Phoenix carefully stepped around Darius and went to the edge of the waterfall. The trees ringing the water were silent and she looked for Alex. There was no sign of him and she crept closer to the edge, listening to the water drip and flow around her.

"Alex?"

"How's Darius? He coming back with Karl?"

Phoenix still couldn't see Alex, but she could hear him. From her vantage point it was difficult to see the entire lagoon. She didn't want to tell him about Darius like this. "Where's the doctor? Where's Max?" she asked.

"He's okay. I found him. He's waiting in the shade. I just wanted to cool off, try and get the smell of shit off me. It's so hot I could—"

There was a sudden noise and Alex went silent. Phoenix crawled further forward to the very edge of the waterfall, praying that Alex was not in trouble. The lagoon was bubbling and foaming beneath the waterfall, and Phoenix looked down. She crawled forward carefully and looked at the water as it swirled around.

"Alex?"

The waterfall had become no more than a trickle so whatever was causing it had to be already in the lagoon. It hit Phoenix like a rocket. She remembered how Justin had died. Something in the water had gotten to him. There was something in the lagoon that had been hiding and waiting for someone to make a mistake. Phoenix scrambled to her feet and pointed to the jungle.

"Alex, get out of the water," Phoenix screamed. She glanced down and saw the bubbling had stopped. From atop the waterfall, she saw a shape in the water, no more than a shadow beneath the surface, but something big. There was no sign of Alex anywhere and Phoenix just hoped she wasn't already too late. She jumped up, trying to spy him below. "Get out, Alex. Now!"

CHAPTER 12

His death was not like the others. When Alex disappeared beneath the water, he simply never came back up. He just slipped under the water without making a noise and never resurfaced. He never screamed or made a sound. There was no time for him to react or escape, only die.

"Alex." Phoenix sank to her knees, ignoring the pain shooting up her leg. She scanned the water for him, but it was as if he had never been there. Whatever had taken him had done it quickly. She had seen a flash of silvery skin burst above the surface and then he was gone. She thought she had seen teeth, long and vicious, but it had all happened so quickly, she wasn't sure of anything. The shape had resembled a crocodile yet its size was more than she could comprehend. There was no way it had just been a regular crocodile. It was another relic, a beast from a different time. It had to live in the lagoon, and yet when she and Karl had been there with Alex earlier, there was no sign of it. How could something so huge live in such a small area? It had to have a cave, perhaps behind the waterfall. All that was left of Alex was a red blood stain running down the water's edge, across some rocks and into the lagoon. The mysterious creature had snatched him when he'd turned his back, and Alex had paid for his miscalculation with his life.

Phoenix looked for the creature, for what had taken him, but the shape disappeared rapidly once it had its prize, and with it so she had lost the third member of her unit. She watched and waited until she knew he wasn't coming back. She thought of jumping in and looking for him, but there was no point. She wouldn't find him, only kill herself in the process. Whatever had taken him would make certain of that.

Hopelessness embraced Phoenix as she stared at the water. What other secrets did this island hide? What else did they have to face? It wasn't fair. This island had kept itself hidden from the world for so long that man wasn't prepared for it or able to deal with what it offered. The creatures that lived here, the unusual vegetation, and the sapping heat were all designed by nature to keep humans away. They had strayed somewhere they shouldn't have and were paying the price. Phoenix tried to think of who to blame. Space54? General Greene? God? *Herself*? It was too easy to apportion blame, and yet none of it sat right. There was nobody to blame. It was just unfortunate circumstances that had led her here. Was it her fault? How could she have known there were dinosaurs on the island? How could anyone have predicted this?

It wasn't entirely fate that had led her here. She had chosen this path. She had chosen a life different to her sisters. Nobody had forced to do this job. Ultimately, she had nobody to blame but herself. She was on the island because she had let herself take this path. Would she be any happier sipping coffee over brunch at book-club? Maybe, but maybe not. She would at least have a better chance of a long life. As she stared at the empty lagoon, she began to doubt they would make the beach. All those doubts she harbored began to flood back in, joining the hopelessness that swam around her head. She had taken on more than she could handle. Karl should be in charge. She had held him back too long. If Karl was in charge, they would have turned around at the first sign of trouble and Darius, Justin, and Alex would still be alive.

"Phoenix? Come on down here," shouted Karl.

He was already at the trees by the lagoon. She could see him scouring the area. Confusion spread over him.

"Where's Alex?" he shouted.

Phoenix stood up and tried to wipe away the self-doubt. It wasn't the first time someone had died under her watch. She knew the procedure. She knew what she had to do. Yet getting herself under control was more difficult than it had ever been before. She felt her hopelessness evaporate and then frustration set in. Three words kept repeating themselves over and over in her head.

It wasn't fair.

People didn't die on tropical islands. Her unit didn't get killed without good reason. Yet both had happened here, today, and she was powerless to do anything about it. As she looked at Karl, she knew she had to tell him. She had to tell him they had lost another one. She had been backed into another corner by this island that looked so idyllic yet was a haven for death. Karl's eyes reached the lagoon where the water had turned thick and red. Phoenix saw him holding Alex' discarded shirt, and as she met his eyes, she knew he understood. She didn't have to say a word. Karl's shoulders slumped.

It wasn't fair.

Anger grew in her veins, spreading like a cancer until it racked her whole body. Phoenix got up and stormed over to the dinosaur. "How... many...more?" she screamed as she punched the beast. Her fists pummeled it until her fingers were bleeding, the skin red raw. The first tear finally fell down her cheek and she wiped it away, ashamed. As she stood back, her chest heaving as she took in deep breaths, she felt dizzy again and forced herself to unclench her fingers. Control. She had to regain control. She had to get back to the beach.

Phoenix jumped up onto the dead dinosaur and climbed back over it, back the way they had come until she reached Karl. He was still standing where she had last seen him, clutching Alex's shirt.

"It took him before I had a chance," said Phoenix weakly as she approached Karl. "I called out to him, but—"

"Damn fool. He didn't listen." Karl dropped Alex's shirt on the ground. A line of ants immediately began to close in on it and the trail of blood leading to the water. "I can't believe... I can't... Let's just get the doc and go home."

Without speaking, Phoenix let Karl lead her to the jungle. There, sat on a rock as if nothing had happened, was Max. He had his hands clasped in front of him and his head lowered as if he were in prayer. She saw several cuts on his face and arms, and as he stood up to greet her, he held out a hand.

"I'm sorry about your men. Truly. It wasn't meant to be like this."

Phoenix waved away his hand. She didn't care what the doctor thought. He wasn't responsible for their deaths, but making small talk was the last thing on her mind. Max was acting as if they were at a wake and half-expecting prawn sandwiches to be offered around.

"Grab your gear, Doc, we're leaving," she said. "We need to get away from that lagoon and whatever monster lives in it." Phoenix watched Karl pull a knife out from his boot. The blade was only a couple of inches long, and it would have no impact if they encountered another dinosaur. She caught Karl's eyes, weary and bloodshot.

"It's all we have left," he offered and held the knife to her. "If you want it, it's yours."

Karl seemed quiet. His bravado was gone. It was as if he was defeated. She hadn't seen him like this since they had lost Sawyer and Travers. Phoenix looked at the jungle. There was nothing she could say to bring him round. There was nothing she could do to make things right. They were going home a failure, the operation a complete disaster and her unit dead. The jungle appeared to be just as unwelcoming as when they had first travelled through it. The path would be quicker if they could retrace their steps, but it would still be a hard slog. The jungle had been given several hours to heat up and they had lost plenty of energy. The only fresh water available to them was from the lagoon, yet it was tainted with the blood of Alex, Justin, and the dinosaur. She wouldn't drink it if it meant the difference between living and dying.

"Keep it."

Karl tucked the knife back in his boot. "Hold on, Doc, there's something we need to do before we set off back to the beach."

"You mean we're leaving, right now?" asked Max. "But what about Jane and Tobias and—?"

"Forget them," said Phoenix calmly. "They're dead. You've seen what we've dealt with today. You should be thinking along the same lines as us, about getting home. Your people are gone, Max."

Max sighed. "You know, we still have a few hours of daylight, and the guide said he wouldn't be back until sundown. I know the situation has taken a turn for the worse, but the monster's dead now. We should take this opportunity to look for my colleagues while we can." Max rifled a hand through his white hair. "Quite frankly, I had heard good things about you, Phoenix. I didn't think you would give up quite so easily."

Karl grabbed Max by the throat and thrust him back until he had him pressed up against the solid trunk of a tree.

"You want to try that again, Doc? You think we're just giving up? We just lost three men. Your people are dead. Phoenix has done everything she could. If it wasn't for her, I would've given up on this wild goose chase long ago. She's the only reason why I haven't knocked your teeth out already."

"How very professional of you." Max was scared. He tried not to show it, but it was obvious. "So, what now? We go home with our tail between our legs?"

"Let go of him, Karl. I can't be bothered to fight with him, not now."

Karl lowered his hands leaving Max rubbing his neck.

"You can stay here or come with us. Honestly, Max, I don't give a shit anymore." Phoenix rolled her shoulders. She refused to let him wind her up. "But one more word out of you the wrong way, and I will let Karl tear you apart."

"Fine." Max grabbed his backpack and tossed it over one shoulder. "I guess we're off then."

"Wait a second." Karl grabbed the doctor's pack off him and threw it to the ground. "Phoenix sit down. As much as I can't stand this asshole, he does have one thing going for him. He's a doctor, and you need attention. You can't walk through that jungle for the next couple of hours with your leg bleeding like that."

Phoenix looked down at her right thigh where the tooth was still protruding through her khakis. The lower half of her pants was soaked with blood. The pain was just a dull throb, but Karl was right. She would slow them down and be no good to anyone if she ended up passing out in the middle of a steamy jungle.

"Fine," she said reluctantly. "Patch me up, Doc, but make it quick. I want out of here."

Phoenix sat down on a rock and stretched out her leg. It was only now, as she took her weight off it, that it began to hurt more.

There had been so much else to do, so much else to occupy her mind that her brain had blocked out the pain.

Max nervously approached Karl. "Give me my bag."

"Sure. Just patch her up," said Karl, holding out the doctor's pack.

Max reached for it. "Look, it's not that easy. The tooth in her leg might've struck an artery. If I pull it out now, we could do more harm than good. I think we're best to wait, get back to the boat and look at it there."

As Max's hand fumbled for his pack, Karl pulled it away. "*No*. You're a doctor, right? Do what you came here for and look at her leg."

"As I said, it's not that simple. I really don't have the right equipment with me. Just hand me my pack and I promise that I will look at it when—"

"Back the fuck up," said Karl as he pushed Max away. He held the pack out of arm's reach, seeing the annoyance on the doctor's face. "Just explain to me why you don't have the necessary equipment. Hm? You should have bandages, sutures, everything you need. You did earlier, so you should have a whole ton of it left."

"He's stalling." Phoenix saw Max glance at her. His eyes betrayed him. "I doubt he's even a doctor."

"Now hold on, I haven't done anything to you. I told you everything I could. Space54 wanted—"

"Yeah, I heard it before, Doc." Karl tossed his pack to Phoenix. "Open it."

"Wait!" Max lunged for his pack, but Karl grabbed him in a bear hug. The doctor struggled, but it was futile. Karl was too strong.

Phoenix felt around inside Max's bag for a bandage, for anything to stop the bleeding. Her hand brushed over something sharp, and for a moment, she worried she had found a needle. Yet as she looked inside the pack, she realized Karl was right. He wasn't even a doctor.

"Doc, what the hell is this?" Phoenix pulled a small rock out of the bag and held it up. It looked completely ordinary, just small and brown with a reddish tinge. She tossed it to the ground and pulled out another one.

"Please, stop. You don't know what you're doing," said Max as he struggled with Karl.

Phoenix tossed the second piece of rock aside and shoved her hand back into the doctor's bag. All she found were more rocks and what felt like gravel. She pulled a handful of the dirt out and let it trickle through her fingers.

"Stop!"

Max burst free of Karl and sank to the ground. He began to collect the dirt in his hands and gather the rocks that Phoenix had tossed away.

Phoenix and Karl looked at each other, bemused.

"You want to explain now?" asked Phoenix, watching the doctor scramble around in the dirt. She shoved her hand back into the doctor's bag. There was nothing. Just more rocks. "This mission was never about the lives of those scientists, was it? This was just a fucking ruse, a play to get you here so you could find your damn satellite."

Max rocked back on his haunches and looked up at Phoenix. He might have been afraid of Karl, but when he looked at her, she saw nothing but contempt.

"It's a probe, actually, not a satellite."

Karl glared menacingly. "You want to play *games*, Max?"

"We came all this way for a bunch of rocks?" asked Phoenix. "Really? For nothing but a bunch of fucking *rocks*?"

Max held up his hands. "You don't understand. The data we got back was incomplete. We needed the physical evidence that we could find water on Mars. These rocks could change the course of mankind, don't you see that? We would never have been able to get them without using you. I had to get here, to find them for myself. There are more out there where the probe landed. If we can just go back and examine it, I can—"

"And you never gave a damn about those three people we came here for. Did you even know them?" asked Phoenix.

Max stood up, holding one of his precious rocks. "Yes, I knew them," he said defensively. "I told you the truth about that. I really did hope we would find them."

"But they were only of secondary importance, right? The real mission here was to retrieve those rocks and your data." Phoenix gritted her teeth and yanked the tooth out of her thigh. She winced as the blood oozed from her leg and dripped between her fingers. "And you're not a doctor, are you?"

Max shook his head. "No. I have some basic training, but I'm an astrogeologist by day. I was just guessing when I tended to Justin earlier. Space54 gave me some basic supplies in case anything came up. They didn't really expect me to be called upon. I can't do anything for your leg. Sorry."

Karl planted a fist on the doctor's jaw and Max tumbled back, falling into the undergrowth. He yelped in pain as Karl leered over him. "That's the least you deserve." Karl turned to Phoenix and tore a strip off his already-ripped shirt. He wrapped it around Phoenix's thigh. "Hold that and press on the wound. We need to stop the bleeding before we start trekking through that jungle."

Phoenix looked at Max. He was sat at the base of the tree nursing a swollen jaw. Somehow, he had managed to keep hold of one of the rocks. To Phoenix, it looked like every other rock she had seen, but she guessed that to Max it was special. She could understand why he had done it, even if she disagreed with him. They never would have gone along with it if they had known the truth. The Yasawas were an unforgiving place for the unprepared, and Space54 had blown their chance to retrieve their probe when the first operation had failed. They would never have been given a second opportunity to come to the island so they had sold it as a rescue operation. It made sense. They had fooled everyone. But they hadn't counted on the dinosaur that lived here. Max was in just as much trouble as she was. If he wanted off the island, he was going to have to join them, not fight them.

"You know we have to take him with us." Phoenix looked at Karl, trying to catch his eyes. He was staring at the lagoon. She knew what he was thinking. That Darius, Alex, and Justin had died for nothing; that they had been ambushed. "He's the only one who can explain this, tell everyone what really happened. You know *we* can't say anything."

"You think when we get to civilization he's going to confess all?" Karl shook his head. "He'll clam up as soon as we're back on the boat."

"Maybe so, but we're not leaving him here." Phoenix tried to ignore the sweat pouring down her back. "*Are we,* Karl?"

Karl knew it wasn't a question. He gave Phoenix a brief nod. "Hold that tight on your leg." He picked up the doctor's bag and began to shove the rocks and stones back inside. When he was done, he looked at Max. "You want these?"

Max got to his feet tentatively and held out his hands. "Yes, please, I've got what I came for, I promise—"

Karl hurled the pack above his head and launched it into the air. There was a splash as it landed in the center of the lagoon.

"Then go get it, asshole. We're leaving. What you do next is up to you."

"No!" Max ran past Karl, dropping the only rock he had left from Mars, and reached the water's edge. "Oh, God, no," he said as the bag slipped beneath the surface.

"Not the most mature thing you've done," said Phoenix, smiling as Karl helped her up.

Karl shrugged. "Let's see just how much those rocks mean to him. If he wants them, he can go where Alex and Justin did and get them. I wonder how much he values his own life over that bag."

CHAPTER 13

Phoenix cautiously put some weight on her leg. Karl's makeshift bandage was wrapped around tightly, and although there was some pain, there it wasn't enough to stop her walking. "I'll be fine," she said, grimacing. "Let's just get to the beach."

Karl put his arm around her shoulder and she shrugged him off.

"I'm *fine*."

"Okay, just don't be a martyr and pass out on me."

"Only if you agree not to be a hero." Phoenix smiled wryly. Karl had no other setting. He led by example. The unit looked up to him, as everyone did. His obvious physical strength was nothing compared to his personality. Phoenix knew she was lucky to have him around. All their differences seemed so trivial now. Ultimately, they wanted the same thing: to lead their team safely into battle and out again. Rarely did it go wrong. They worked well together, despite the bickering and irritations. And she had to admit that she had been impressed when he'd punched Max for her. It wasn't the right thing to do, but boy was she glad he'd done it. "You can lead the way. If you remember, I didn't end up here the same way as you did. I don't know what direction to go. You can take the lead and try to get us on the same path back. I'll be right behind you."

Karl looked at Max. He was skirting around the lagoon's edge, red water splashing on his boots. His pack was nowhere in sight.

"And him?"

Phoenix looked at Max. She couldn't bring herself to hate him. He was doing his job, just what Space54 wanted him to do.

Was it his fault that her unit had been decimated? Was it his fault he had ended up in this position? She thought back to the hillside when they had been looking for clues, for the survivors. There had been a brief period when Max had gone missing. That must be when he had collected the samples. He had found what he had come for and now it was gone. There was a small part of her that felt sorry for him. He had failed in his mission, as she had failed in hers. But it was only a very small part of her. There would be more probes, more missions into space. They could send up another rocket and replace their missing data. Replacing Alex, Darius, and Justin was impossible; to her, their lives were worth a million rocks from Mars.

"Max, either go fishing or follow us," shouted Phoenix. "We're leaving."

She suspected that Max would prefer to live than be marooned on a dinosaur-infested island for the rest of his very short life, and he began to trudge toward her with a heavy face.

"You can't do this," he said. "The contents of that bag are invaluable."

"And so is my life, Doc. Deal with it."

Phoenix nodded to Karl and he walked into the jungle, pushing aside vines and branches. Phoenix followed him, trying not to limp, trying not to let him see her pain. The heat of the island changed once they were under the jungle's canopy. The atmosphere changed with it. Karl and Max were only a few feet from her at any time, yet as she walked toward her old life, she couldn't help but think that the island was dead. The inner island at least felt suffocating. The heat was oppressive, and there was no bird-song or sign of animal life now, only the odd bug to freak her out. There had been a bird back at the lagoon, but it was rare to see any life on the island. The further they walked, the darker it got. Sunlight broke through, occasionally striking her face like lightning, but mostly they trudged on in silence and darkness. The sweltering heat made it feel like they were walking through a giant oven, their flesh sizzling as if on a spit-roast. There was no breeze, no blue sky; even the plants were dark, their leaves the color of copper and old coins. Phoenix swept thick, vein-filled leaves aside that were as large as the boat they had arrived on, covered in bugs and spiders the size of meatballs.

"This is ridiculous," muttered Max behind her. "He had no right to do that."

Phoenix ignored him. His protestations continued for a while, coming a few minutes apart. It seemed that the more she ignored him, the quieter he got, realizing she wasn't going to bite. She knew he was pissed off, but he would accept soon that his treasure was gone. They hadn't come here looking for gold, but for people, for life. All they had found was death.

They eventually reached a clearing and Phoenix recognized the dead tree in its center. It was where they had first encountered the dinosaur. Huge footprints had been left in the ground, and many of the surrounding trees had been ripped apart by the hail of bullets her unit had unleashed upon the monster. Remembering how close she had been to it was a reminder of how dangerous the island could be. As Karl paused, she sat down on the dead trunk, grateful for the rest. Karl was looking around the clearing, apparently looking for something, though she couldn't guess what.

"Lost?" Max stood next to Phoenix but addressed Karl. "Guess you don't know everything after all."

Phoenix looked up at the doctor. He had stood by her for protection, knowing Karl was less likely to strike him if he was out of range. "Unless you want another fist to the face, I suggest you keep your opinions to yourself. Trust me, the usual rules of this operation are over. Karl and I are on the same page now. And if he wants to give your face a makeover, I am *not* in the mood to stop him."

Max scuffed his feet and walked away, muttering under his breath. Karl came over to Phoenix and sat down quietly.

"What is it?" she asked. "You know where we are, right?"

"Yeah, I know."

Karl looked around the trees. Phoenix could see he was anxious, but as far as she could tell, there was nothing to be worried about. The dinosaur was dead, and whatever was in the lagoon was clearly behind them, confined to its aquatic home.

"So?"

Karl looked around. Max was within earshot but pretending he wasn't listening to every word they said.

"There's something out there. Something in the jungle."

Phoenix could feel her body tense up. She dug her fingers into the bark by her legs. "What is it? You sure?"

Karl nodded. Sweat gleamed on his forehead. "I think it's tracking us. I noticed a few minutes back. I'm not sure what though. I don't think it's like the dino we already found. This is smaller. Careful. It might be checking us out."

"Seeing if we're good enough for supper?"

Karl put his hands on his neck. His skin was burnt and hot. "Maybe."

They watched the trees for sign of movement but not even a leaf stirred. Phoenix felt something crawl up her arm and she brushed it away without looking. She didn't want to know what it was.

"Are we just going to sit here and wait to be attacked?" asked Max. "Don't you think we should be *doing* something?"

"Such as?" Phoenix kicked her feet around in the dirt and pulled out a small stone that fit comfortably into the palm of her hand.

"Like, I don't know, how about getting to the beach?"

"Nobody's stopping you, Max," replied Phoenix. "Go ahead. The trail's over there somewhere, but I'm sure you'll pick it up."

Max hesitated.

"Thought so." Phoenix knew Max well enough by now to know he was ultimately a coward. He wouldn't go anywhere without them, without his underpaid bodyguards. They were his only ticket home, and Max might be afraid, but he wasn't stupid enough to go walking through a dinosaur-infested jungle on his own.

"Look," said Karl suddenly, gripping Phoenix's arm. "Look there."

A few feet away, behind the lush vegetation growing around the clearing, something stirred. Phoenix looked for the tell-tale blue eyes and listened for the roar, but all she saw was a stirring of the shadows in the hazy heat.

"What do we do now?" whispered Max. "Should we run for it?"

Karl put himself between Phoenix and the jungle. "Too late for that now. Whatever it is, it knows we're here. It's coming."

A memory shook Phoenix then as she remembered Mosul. They were pinned down and Sawyer had been taken out. His body lay in the dust, blood pouring into the dry dirt from the bullet holes in his body. Karl had shoved Phoenix without warning behind him, grabbing her arm then as he had now. Back then, she had let him. She had pretended not to notice, but death had seemed so imminent, so real and all around her, that she had let him. He had been protecting her and instinctively was doing the same now. She wished she could say something to him, but Karl was a different species. She would discuss carbine rifles with him, but the merest mention of a private life or emotion, and he would change the subject. She also knew she couldn't let him protect her any longer. It was time she faced up to whatever was out there.

"Karl, watch Max. Make sure he gets back to the boat. He's our responsibility, unfortunately for us, until we're back on American soil." Phoenix marched past Karl to the jungle. She approached the trees warily. She couldn't see anything through the low-hanging branches and vines. The nearest bush had grown larger than a man, and there was a spider's web drooping from one corner. Whatever creature was preparing to pounce on them was going to have to get through her first. She held the stone in her hand firmly. She might get a chance to use it, she might not. But she sure as hell was through being pushed around and dictated to. It was time she took charge of her own destiny. "Let's get this over with."

"Phoenix, don't be—" began Karl, but he stopped short when the figure emerged from the trees.

"Holy hell," muttered Max.

Phoenix watched as the spider's web was destroyed and the vines parted. A dark figure stepped through. They were caked in mud from head to toe and walked barefoot. At first, she thought it was a mirage or a trick of the light. No way was there anyone living on the island. The figure walked slowly and stepped out into the clearing. Phoenix looked them up and down, the stone in her hand still ready to bash in the mysterious person's brains. It seemed as if everything on this island was out to get them. Was this one of Freddy's friends? Was this one of Karl's cannibals?

The figure slowly raised their hands and wiped the mud away from their eyes. It was as if they were made of it and it clung to their body like a second skin. When they had done wiping their face, Phoenix saw two light-blue sad eyes looking at her. They were staring right at her, but the person made no sound. Phoenix realized that if it weren't for the mud, they would be practically naked. There was only a flimsy cotton shirt and shorts to cover them. Some of the mud was covered in dried blood. As Phoenix looked them over, so shocked to see another living person on the island, another realization hit her: it was a woman.

"Jane? Is... is that you?" asked Max.

Phoenix dropped the stone and caught Jane as she fell. "Karl, help me."

Phoenix managed to get her arms under Jane's body before she hit the ground and Karl darted forward to help. Together they gently lowered her to the ground. Phoenix wished she had some water for her, but they had nothing. They had lost all of their gear and had no way of transporting water even if they could find any fresh enough to drink. As Phoenix laid Jane down on the jungle floor, she felt guilty. She should have been thinking how amazing it was she was alive. She should have been grateful to have found even one person alive. Yet all she could think was that she wished it had been one of her own unit. She had been wishing the person was Darius, Alex, or Justin.

"Careful." Karl positioned himself by Jane's head and sat down cross-legged. He nestled her head in his lap as Phoenix and Max knelt down beside her.

"Jane, is that really you?" asked Max. "I can't believe it. What happened? Where are the others? Jane, what happened?"

"Back off, Max, give her some space," ordered Phoenix. She glared at Max and he shut up.

Phoenix rubbed Jane's hand. She was still conscious, but her eyelids were slowly closing and she seemed to be having trouble focusing. Phoenix spoke in a soothing tone, lowering her voice. She spoke to Jane as if she were a sick child. "Jane, stay with us.

You're okay. We're here to help you, okay honey? Just look at me, look at my eyes, okay? That's right, that's good. My name is Phoenix and the man with me is Karl. We're with the Army. We came for *you*, Jane. We found you. You'll be okay now. Just stay with me. Talk to me, Jane."

Eventually, she seemed to come around. Jane's eyes drifted back to Phoenix and she licked her lips. They were dry and cracked. It took every ounce of effort just to speak.

"Please... water?"

Phoenix smiled apologetically. "Sorry, we're all out, but we'll try to get you some. I'm sorry, Jane, we had a little trouble finding you." She looked up at Karl who was casually running his fingers through Jane's hair. Phoenix remembered how he had a daughter, how he was once married and had probably done the same thing with them. It was odd seeing him like that. He had always been decent and done his best for other people, but his nurturing side rarely showed itself. "Jane, it's going to be okay. We have a boat. We can get you out of here. It's not far. Just through the jungle. Just relax and let us help you."

"Jane, did you find it? Did you manage to retrieve any of the—?"

"Max," hissed Phoenix, "I'm not going to tell you again."

The heat of the jungle dripped around them and Phoenix suddenly felt trapped. How were they going to get Jane out of there if she couldn't walk? They had no water or food. They had no weapons if they were attacked again, apart from Karl's small knife. Time was not on their side, and Phoenix knew they had to keep moving. It didn't matter about the damn rocks or the probe. Max had lost his chance. There were four lives in the balance. Phoenix only had to find out one thing before they could move on.

"Jane, where are Tobias and Ricardo? Are they here?" Phoenix felt Jane tense up. She suddenly avoided making eye contact with anyone and pushed herself into an upright position.

"Jane?" asked Karl, looking at Phoenix. "We're here to help you. We need to know who else is on this island."

Jane scratched at her throat, picking off pieces of mud. She pulled at some that had dried around her shoulders. Phoenix suspected that underneath all that dirt and fear and shame was an attractive young woman. If the men were with her, they would have shown themselves by now. As they weren't, that meant they were probably dead. Phoenix had enough experience to know that assumptions out in the field could lead to disastrous consequences. She had to know for sure. She had to hear it from Jane.

Jane cleared her throat. "It happened... it happened so fast."

Phoenix noticed that underneath the slime and dirt, Jane had blonde hair. She was a natural too. The girl began to look younger by the minute as more of the mud fell off her. She reminded Phoenix of her sister, Virginia. She was blonde and naturally pretty too. She had settled down in Oklahoma, not far from the family home, with a nice guy, an accountant. Phoenix missed home. She missed her sisters. She missed normal life, not that she'd had enough of it to know what 'normal' really meant. There was no mud or flies or dirt in real life. There were no dinosaurs in normal life. She had been fighting for so long that she had forgotten what it must be like to live a normal life. Jane probably had one back home. She had somehow survived on this island, made it further than half of her unit had. Yet she looked fragile and scared. How had she done it? Phoenix felt the urge to hold her, as if she were holding Virginia, as if by being close to her she could somehow get a piece of that normal life for herself. Like Max, Jane was under her wing, her responsibility now. She was going to get her home. She was going to get them all home.

"Go on," said Phoenix warmly. "Go on, Jane. Take your time. What happened to you?"

CHAPTER 14

"I think Tobias and Ricardo were actually enjoying themselves. I couldn't believe I was on this amazing island with them even though I was sick as a dog. The journey over and the heat was a little too much for me. The chief and his tribe were so friendly and welcoming when we got here. They made sure we understood what we were allowed to do, and what was off limits. By the time we actually made it to the island, my stomach was doing somersaults. I tried to ignore it. I wanted to be part of it. I didn't want to admit I was sick and go home empty handed. I didn't want to go back to the boat with nothing. Our guide, Freddy, had such a nice smile. I remember that. He was nice."

Phoenix remembered Freddy too and wondered if he was typical of the local tribe. It appeared so, if Jane was right about how friendly they were. She didn't want to distract Jane from her story though so she kept quiet, letting Jane do the talking.

"We hacked our way through the jungle until Tobias found something. It was just a piece of metal, but it was from the probe. We'd picked up its trajectory and thought we could find it. We estimated it was somewhere on the peak, in an area we could reach. We could almost feel it in our hands. Tobias found a small piece of the hull. It put us on the right track. For a while anyway. We came to a clearing quite like this. Probably not too far away. The island isn't big, but when you're stuck here, it doesn't feel it; there aren't many places to hide. When you're trying to hide from those things, then it seems like the island is tiny."

Things. Phoenix could guess what she was talking about: the dinosaur they had killed and the one trapped in the lagoon.

"Tobias had scouted up ahead and climbed a tree to look for the probe. It was up on a hillside. It was in pieces, but he was hopeful we would be able to retrieve something from the crash site."

"I found it, Jane," said Max eagerly. "I found it. I got the samples, except—"

"It didn't work out," said Phoenix. She didn't want him and Karl to get into anything again. "The probe and samples are gone. Tell me what happened, Jane. Where are the others?"

Jane swallowed nervously. "It got Tobias first. He was so happy, so excited and then… the monster got him. It was hiding in the trees. It can camouflage itself in the jungle so you don't even know it's there until it's right on top of you. It was huge and these two bright blue eyes just stare at you. I don't really know how to describe it. We thought the island was uninhabited. Freddy said that nobody lived here and I can see why. This place is full of ghosts. That monster killed Tobias, just plucked him right out of the tree and started eating him in front of us."

"Jesus," whispered Max. "Poor Tobias."

Now he gets a conscience, thought Phoenix, *or is he playing pretend again so he can get more information out of Jane? Does he still think he can get something out of this place?*

"Then it came for us," continued Jane. "I convinced Ricardo we should run for it. There was some tall grass nearby, and if we'd stayed it would have quickly attacked us, I'm sure of it. So we ran. We ran for the grass, to hide, and that's when it got Ricardo. One second I was running right next to him and then, whoosh, he was gone, up into the air, up into that thing's jaws. It could so easily have been me, but I made it to the grass. I made it far enough to escape, but I wanted to wait for Ricardo. I kept thinking maybe if he could get away from it, he might still be okay, might still be able to get me off this island. I heard him screaming. He… he took a long time to die."

Phoenix listened to Jane's story, amazed that this young girl was still holding it together. As she spoke, she kept her emotions in check. Phoenix wasn't sure if that was part of her survival mechanism or just because she didn't have the energy for anything else. The more she spoke about what had happened to her the more she seemed to wake up, which was good. Soon, they were going to have to go if they were to make the rendezvous with Freddy.

"I kept walking. I just kept walking further into the jungle away from that monster. I had no idea where I was going or what I was going to do. All I knew was that I had to put as much distance as possible between myself and that thing. What was it? Do you know? You must have worked it out before you killed it, right?"

Phoenix was surprised when Jane admitted she knew that it was dead. "You saw it die? You know what happened to us?"

"Not exactly. I heard the explosion. And you're still here. I put two and two together when I saw you." Suddenly, Jane sat bolt upright and opened her eyes. "Oh my God, you did kill it, didn't you? Tell me it's dead. I don't think I can handle—"

"It's dead," confirmed Karl. "Don't worry, it's deader than corduroy."

Jane looked confused. "Corduroy? What's that?"

Phoenix smirked. "Never mind Grandad; he still thinks cellphones have buttons. Focus on the fact that it's dead now, Jane. We think it was some sort of dinosaur, a relic from the past that somehow lived on this private island away from man. My guess is that it didn't even know what a human was when it saw one for the first time. To that monster, we were just something else to eat."

Phoenix asked if Jane could stand, and with her reassured about the dead dinosaur, they got her to her feet.

"Can you walk? We need to move soon."

"I'll be okay now. I'm sorry about surprising you before. I just kind of stumbled across you by accident really. After Tobias and Ricardo were killed, I wandered around for hours, completely lost. I heard the monster, the dinosaur, occasionally trampling through the jungle or roaring. It didn't find me. I tried to get back to the beach that first day, but I never found it again. I came to a few small coves, but there was nothing there. There was no way off the island, no way to signal for help. I had my pack but went through the rations way too fast. I was stupid. I should've saved them, but I figured I wouldn't be here long. I tried to record what was happening too. I took some video on the tablet they gave us, but the dinosaur found me. It tore the pack right off my back and I dropped everything. I got lucky twice. After that, I just had to hope that Freddy, our guide, would report us as lost. I was hoping rescue would come, but I didn't figure that it would take you this long to find me."

"Yeah, I guess the dinosaur kind of put a crimp in our plans for that," said Phoenix. "How did you manage to survive for so long? I'm impressed, Jane. You must have quite a story."

Karl tapped his wrist at an imaginary watch. "You know, we really should start moving. Jane's missed the boat once, and I'm sure she doesn't want to miss it again."

"Right, true. Jane, if you're okay, then we're going to leave. Karl can lead us back to the beach. You're going to be okay now."

"Sure, but just one thing. Wait one second." Jane disappeared back into the jungle from where she had emerged, and Phoenix heard the bushes rustle for a moment before Jane returned with two machetes. They were covered in mud too. "Here," said Jane as she handed one to Phoenix and one to Karl. "Sorry I didn't bring them out earlier. I wasn't entirely sure you were on my side. I kind of lost myself for a little back there."

"Are you freaking kidding me?" asked Karl with a grin on his face. He held up the machete to the sunlight. "I could kiss you, Jane."

"Steady on, Karl." Phoenix felt the satisfying weight of the machete in her hand. It felt better to be armed. Just in case. Even with the dinosaur dead, Phoenix knew she wouldn't feel completely safe until they were back on the helicopter and headed for the Reagan. "Where the hell did you get *these*?"

"We brought them with us," announced Jane. "I dropped mine when the dinosaur attacked, but I managed to retrieve it earlier today. The other I found the next day. It was Ricardo's."

"We're not *completely* stupid," said Max. "We gave Jane and the others enough to survive out here. We tried to do it right, didn't we, Jane?"

"Sure. Space54 didn't know what this place was really like."

Phoenix knew Max was trying to cover himself. He was already starting to make out he was on their side, as if he was part of the rescue operation. He wanted Jane on his side, and if there was time, he would try to find out where he could get more of those precious rocks. Phoenix had no intention of letting him get away with it that easily.

"Max, follow Karl and stay in sight. I think it's time we got out of here. And I'm sure you have a million questions for Jane, but she's going to walk with me. Got that?"

Max looked annoyed but agreed to it. He had no choice. Now that Phoenix and Karl had the machetes, she felt much better about leading them back into the jungle. They trudged on slowly as Karl attempted to retrace their path back to the beach.

"You know, Jane, I think you did something amazing here. We'd all but given up on you. How did you manage to evade the dinosaur until we got here?" asked Phoenix. Her leg was sore and the wound where the dinosaur had bit her had opened up. She could feel blood slowly dripping down the inside of her pants. Yet if she admitted that to Karl, he would insist on stopping and attending to it. They didn't have the time for anything now but getting to the beach.

"That first night was horrible. I found a small cave by the seashore to shelter in, but I was freezing. I had no way of making a fire and nothing to eat or drink. I lay there for hours trying to sleep, but it was difficult. I was nearly bitten to death by the sandflies. The only way I could stop them was to cover myself in mud. It took me until the second night to figure that out. I covered myself head to toe in it and they stopped bothering me."

That at least explained why she was covered in dirt, thought Phoenix.

"The second day, I concentrated at first on finding something to eat or drink. I knew I had to hold on until they sent another boat or someone to find me. In the morning, I walked back into the jungle. I didn't find much. No fruit or anything that looked like food to me. I did find a bush close to a lagoon with some berries on. They looked good, but they tasted foul. I only ate a couple and I knew they were bad. I didn't find anything else. All these trees and plants and no fruit anywhere; not even a coconut or mango tree. I lost my appetite around lunchtime when I stumbled across Ricardo's remains.

"There wasn't really much left of him. The monster had either eaten or taken most of him. I picked up his machete which was still in his hands. I searched the area and found a power bar that he must have had on him. I gobbled it down in two seconds flat. I'm not even joking. It's all I've had to eat for days. And of course, by then, the heat was draining me of what little energy I had. I guess I knew I just had to keep going. I tried not to think about what would happen if I ran into that thing again. I had to find water so I kept walking, hoping I would find something."

"Did you?"

"Yes, but it almost cost me my life. There was a lagoon further inland. I just fell to my knees when I found it and drank. Luckily, I was still on edge, waiting for the dinosaur to attack again, and I noticed the water change. I pulled away and saw something in the water. It was something else, just as big as my monster, but different. It just looked at me. It poked its head above the water and looked right at me. I didn't go back after that. I knew it wasn't safe. I went back to the beach and scoured the ocean for hours looking for a passing boat. I waited until it was dark and then went back to my cave. I didn't sleep that good, even though the sandflies left me alone. I was tired and hungry and, I hate to say it, I was ready to give up. It just felt like I'd been abandoned, you know? I've got four brothers who look out for me back home, and it was weird being on my own. It was like there was nobody looking out for me anymore. I doubted that rescue was coming when I woke up on the third day. Then I saw something. I grabbed my two machetes and ran inland. I knew I had to get to higher ground, even risk confronting that dinosaur if I had to."

That's when we arrived, thought Phoenix. "When you heard the explosion, did you realize it was us? Did you try to find us?"

"I figured it was something unnatural, something man-made. But truthfully, I wasn't thinking straight by that point. I had no idea what it was. I saw the smoke and guessed someone had taken on that dinosaur and probably beaten it. But I didn't actually find you until a few minutes ago. I was just walking through the jungle hoping I would find whoever had made all that noise and then I heard you talking."

Phoenix stopped walking. Karl and Max had reached a dead-end. The trees swarmed around them in a cluster.

Max winkled his face in disgust. "We should go back. We're not going to make it through this."

Exposed tree roots lay before them, gnarled and twisted, intertwined with long vines that covered the jungle floor.

"We'll find the path again," said Karl.

"This will take too much time and too much energy," replied Max. "We should go back. If we go up the hill to where Jane saw the probe, then maybe we can signal for help. Get one of those military choppers to come get us. It makes sense, right, Jane? You want to get off this island, don't you?"

"Fucking right I do," said Jane, making Phoenix smile as she cursed.

"So, let's go," insisted Max. "It's obvious we need to find the probe so we can—"

"No, Max, it's obvious that nothing had changed for you. Nothing we've said or done has sunk in, has it?" Phoenix sighed. "Get this through your thick skull. The probe is gone. Your rocks are gone. We *are* going to follow Karl to the beach."

"But the dinosaur is dead. It's fucking *dead*. We can get up the hillside easily. We can—"

"You don't get to talk anymore," said Karl, pushing the doctor forward roughly. "Discussion over," he said, waving the machete menacingly in Max's direction.

"Imbeciles."

"Ignore him," said Phoenix, rolling her eyes. Max would never change. He didn't give a damn about his people. Even with Jane in such a fragile state, he still cared more about finding his probe. The man had no scruples. Thankfully, Karl heeded her advice and ignored him. There was a distinctly uncomfortable atmosphere between them as they walked on. The heavy heat didn't help. They all were nursing their own wounds, even Max, and Phoenix just hoped that Karl would get them back soon or they were all liable to start dropping like flies.

Karl found a way around the trees and tried to get them back on the path. The machete he held came in useful when a thick vine got in their way, but he couldn't start chopping down trees with it. He was tired of the island, tired of Max, and tired of constantly fighting. He thought about Justin, Alex, and Darius as he walked.

He remembered what they had been through. With Jane joining them, it didn't seem like it had been such a waste now. If they could get her off the island, then at least something positive had come out of the day. Occasionally, his thoughts slipped to his daughter, but he preferred not to think about her. It was painful being separated from her so often, so he buried her in the back of his mind. He didn't even talk to Phoenix about her even though he was bursting to. He had more than just respect for Phoenix and had long thought about taking things further. He knew she would never go for it and he kept her at bay, constantly sniping and undermining her. As he walked through the jungle, he wondered why he did it. Why couldn't he just be honest and tell her how much she meant to him? The jungle took his mind off all that. It was hard work getting back to the original path that they had carved out and he trained himself to ignore the painful thoughts in his head. He was a soldier and a professional, and he had a job to do.

They pressed on, the ever-thickening jungle encroaching on them as they moved forward. Thick branches snapped at their faces and tendrils of green coiled around their ankles. The jungle tried to hold them back, to protect its secrets from escaping. Phoenix found the pain in her body numbed as she pressed on. As Jane lapsed into weary silence, Phoenix focused on what she would say when they got back to base. Not getting to the beach and the rendezvous with Freddy didn't enter her mind. She couldn't allow that little nugget of negativity to gain any traction in her mind. So, she thought about how she would convince her superiors that she had lost three men to a dinosaur. It wasn't going to be an easy conversation.

"Damn it."

Karl exclaimed and Phoenix saw him standing by a thin tree, its bark covered in small blue flowers. They seemed to sprout from the tree itself. Ivy wound around the trunk right into the upper branches. The flowers were tiny and each one had four large petals containing a red reed-like center.

"Watch yourself," said Karl, "that thing is sharp." He dabbed at a long cut running along his forearm.

The flowers looked attractive, but Phoenix was worried they may contain a foreign toxin that could be deadly. The island contained all sorts of life that man was never meant to encounter.

"We should stop, Karl, and look at that cut." She touched his shoulder gently. "You don't want an infection that—"

"No, I'm not stopping now." Karl didn't want Phoenix to see him vulnerable. He had hidden himself for years from her and had no intention of changing now. He had almost changed his mind back at the lagoon, when he had been tending to her wounds. When he had been holding her face and looking into her eyes, he had been close to kissing her. The idea was ridiculous. She only put up with him because they worked together. She had no more feelings for him than she did a stranger. His arm hurt, but he knew it was no more than her leg. He could tell she was hiding it. They weren't stopping for anything. He didn't trust the island and wanted off. He wanted Phoenix off it before there were any further nasty surprises. He knew that he had to be a good boy and soldier on.

Karl marched on through the jungle, retracing their route as best as he could remember back to the beach. Phoenix followed obligingly knowing there was nothing she could say to deter him or make him stop. Max and Jane remained silent, not even talking to each other. Even though it was getting late, the heat didn't seem to change. Jane had said the temperature dropped at night, but Phoenix guessed that wasn't until the sun went down. By that time, she hoped to be far, far away.

After a while, Karl approached some thick vines that had clumped together and he pulled them aside like a pair of velvety green curtains. What lay ahead made Phoenix gasp. She could hardly believe it. Barely fifty feet ahead of them was the ocean, a rich blue plateau with gently cresting waves rippling the surface.

"We've made it," said Max. "We did it."

Karl held the vines to one side and Phoenix passed through the opening. She noticed that his arm that had been cut by the blue flowers was bruised and the open sore was weeping.

"We need to get that looked at," she said as she stepped out of the darkness of the jungle into sunlight.

"Right after you get your leg seen to," he replied.

Phoenix knew Karl would make sure everyone else was okay before he got himself checked over.

"I mean it. That looks nasty."

Karl just smiled at her and allowed Max and Jane through. They were all bathed in glorious sunshine. It was late in the afternoon, but they had made it. Phoenix recognized the beach. They weren't in the exact spot where Freddy had agreed to pick them up, but they were close. They had emerged from the jungle into a small bay. Shallow water trickled over the coral and to the east there was a rocky outcrop jutting out to sea. A few palm trees fringed the other side and she could see through to the next beach. That was where Freddy would find them. He wouldn't be far away. The sun was in no danger of setting just yet, but she didn't doubt he would come for them. Phoenix breathed an audible sigh of relief.

It was over.

CHAPTER 15

"We did it, Jane, we got you out." Max stretched out his arms as if literally worshipping the sun. "It was hard, but we did it."

Jane slumped to her knees, and Phoenix wondered if she was going to faint.

"Now he wants to be a hero?" Karl unbuttoned his shirt—what was left of it—and tossed it aside. "What's this '*we*' business?"

Phoenix couldn't help but look at Karl's body. His daily workout was paying dividends. Even though he was undeniably attractive, there had never been anything more between them. The thought had crossed her mind on more than one occasion, but he had never shown any interest so she accepted it for what it was. They worked together and that was it, no more, no less. This operation had brought them closer but it would never be more than cordial. She had wondered sometimes about him, wanted him to open up, but it had never happened for some reason. He had spent so much time and effort on undermining her that she assumed he just had a general dislike for her, not that it ever affected their work.

"Admiring the guns, huh?"

Phoenix shook her head. "Dream on, Karl. I'm just worried about your arm."

Karl shrugged. "Whatever. We're here. We made it. That's the beach, right? Freddy will be here soon and we'll be off this stinking island forever. Good riddance to it."

"Don't suppose any of you have a secret stash of Twinkies? I'm starved," said Jane.

Phoenix could see she was struggling. She hadn't eaten anything of sustenance for days.

"All I brought was a six-pack." Karl nudged Phoenix and laughed.

"Oh, God, really?" Phoenix smiled back at him. She couldn't help but glance at his athletic body. "That's what we're reduced to? Your bad jokes? We really are in trouble."

"Come on," said Max. "Quit messing around. We need to get around the bay to the beach. I don't want to miss that boat. I need to get Jane back, get her some medical help and decent food."

"Remember that advice I gave you about not talking?" Karl took a step toward Max. "You might pay to remember that."

"Please. I don't have to take orders from you," replied Max. Suddenly, he had found his confidence again. It had resurfaced now that they were safe, knowing they would very soon be back on the boat and away from the confines of the island. "My priority now is Jane."

"Is that so? And does she know what your priority was while Phoenix and I were looking for her?" Karl took another step across the warm sand to Max. "Does she know how long you spent looking for her? Tell her. Tell her why you came here, Max."

Phoenix looked at Jane. She was exhausted and scared. She could barely stand, yet it was still a long journey back by boat and then helicopter to the *USS Reagan*.

"Maybe we should save this conversation for another time, Karl." Phoenix put a hand on Jane's shoulder. "Let's concentrate on—"

"No, I want to hear this asshole admit it. After the trouble that he's caused us, the people who have died because of him, I want to hear him tell the truth. Just for once, tell the damn truth. Tell her." Karl took another step toward Max. He was within striking distance now. "*Tell her.*"

"Max?" Jane looked up at him, her eyes searching his for answers. "What's he talking about? You came here for me, right? For Tobias and Ricardo. I knew Space54 would send help. Where's the boat? We shouldn't hang around here for long." Jane looked around the beach nervously. "We're too exposed to wait for long."

Max bit his lip and said nothing.

"It's okay, Jane," said Phoenix soothingly. "You're right. We came here for you. And you made it. God knows you must be strong to have survived this long, but you made it. That's what counts. Just rest up, okay?" Phoenix looked at the shadows being cast by the jungle on the beach behind her. "It might be another hour before our ride shows up. I'm not sure of the time anymore. You can sit here and rest. Talk with me. We'll keep an eye out for the boat. Don't worry."

"An *hour*?" Jane seemed to get paler. "Do we have to wait that long?"

"Fuck it." Karl pushed past Max and glared at Phoenix.

"Where are you going?" Phoenix knew he was angry with her, but she had to protect Jane. It would do her no good to hear how Space54 had abandoned her or that Max was a fraud. There would be plenty of time for that later.

"To cool off," replied Karl as he stormed away.

Phoenix knew he wanted to have it out with Max, but the timing wasn't right. "Karl, please don't—"

It was too late. He was striding toward the ocean. Let him go. Maybe he did need to cool off. It had been difficult for him, losing the unit the way they had.

"Jane," said Phoenix turning to her, "it's going to be okay. Trust me. Freddy will be here soon. We can see the beach from here. I'm sure we'll hear his engine coming long before we actually see him. If you prefer, we can go down to the water and—"

"*No*. We're better off here I guess."

"I'm going to the beach," announced Max. "I think we should go and make sure Freddy doesn't miss us. I'd hate to have gotten this far and miss him."

"Max, you don't have to do that, we can see from here. We're not going to miss him."

"What if he misses us? What if he doesn't come back? What if that dinosaur was some sort of God to those people and he deliberately left us here as some kind of sacrifice? Don't you—?"

She couldn't help it. Phoenix whirled to face him with the machete still in her hand. She didn't even realize what she was doing.

"For fuck's sake, Max, quit your whining! Are you serious? You think we were abandoned here on purpose? If you stand in front of me any longer spouting that garbage, I'm liable to sacrifice you myself."

Phoenix was trembling with rage. She followed Max' eyes to her hand and realized she was holding the machete up as if she were about to chop him down. Max was scared, probably more scared than when Karl had hit him.

"Get out of my sight," said Phoenix, unrepentant. She hadn't intentionally threatened him but it was done. If she had scared him into shutting up, then perhaps it would be worth it. "Go, before I call Karl back. You're skating on thin ice, Max."

Max said nothing but turned his back on her and traipsed off in the direction of the beach where he could wait for Freddy alone. Phoenix watched him walk away and lowered her machete. Had she taken it too far? Had she crossed a line? He was a civilian after all and under her responsibility.

"He always was a dick," said Jane quietly.

Phoenix looked at Karl. He was striding into the gentle surf and relaxing in the water. She felt like joining him, just swimming out into the ocean with him and not looking back, but she had Jane to worry about now.

"You knew him well?" asked Phoenix. Karl and Max would have to keep. She could apologize to Karl later. She knew that he thought she was picking sides when really all she was trying to do what keep the peace. She sat down on the stony beach next to Jane. "Back at Space54?"

"Not that well. We were in different buildings. But he was known around the complex. Always had an opinion, always seemed to be picking a fighting with someone. I take it you guys didn't get along?"

Phoenix laughed. "You could say that." It really was all over now. They had lost their own men but had brought back one survivor. Quite what Jane's story was going to be, she didn't know, but that wasn't her department. The military and Space54 no doubt had already cooked up a cover story. Jane would be a hero, and there would be no mention of dinosaurs or anything else unusual. Phoenix and her unit had never been here. They would just go back to work and the world would never know what they had done. Max would go back to his work, prepare for another mission to Mars. Karl would go back to being Karl and she would replenish her depleted unit. There would be some story about a training accident and their families would receive a letter from the president. Life would go back to normal. But could she?

Phoenix had to admit she had felt a change inside of her. Seeing Freddy had made her think of what she had been missing out on. Even Karl had changed too. He had shown her that he wasn't just a soldier but a real man. He had taken care of her on the island. He was a good man but strictly off-limits. She knew practically nothing about his life outside the military. She had only ever seen a picture of his daughter once. Maybe that was part of his act too, the strong and silent type. She still wondered if Karl cared more for her than he let on. Asking him directly would get her nowhere. She was going to have to get him drunk and see where things led when they got back to base.

"Maybe we should go with Max. You said the boat would be here soon, right?" asked Jane.

Phoenix stifled a yawn. Suddenly, she felt exhausted. It had been one of those days. She watched Karl swimming up and down near the beach. He glanced back and waved at her. She smiled and waved back. "Yes," she told Jane, "any time now. I think we'll be fine as soon as—"

"Fuck. Oh no, not now," said Jane. She jumped to her feet. "*Fuck, fuck, fuck.*"

"What is it? What's wrong?" Phoenix grabbed her machete and scrambled to stand. Jane was staring out at the ocean, but Phoenix couldn't see that anything was wrong. "Are you hurt?"

Jane took a slow step back toward the jungle, her eyes never leaving the ocean. "It's here," she said timidly.

Phoenix felt shivers run up her spine. She looked at the ocean but couldn't see a thing. Perhaps Jane was suffering from shock, freaking out now that they were so close to going home. "Jane, what is it? There's nothing there. Why don't you sit down?"

Jane looked around the beach and spied Karl's machete that he had dropped before going to swim. She grabbed it and clutched it to her chest. "I never told you what I saw that morning on the beach. It was that thing. It's here."

"What's here, Jane? You're scaring me." Phoenix looked around her but saw nothing. She listened for a roar, but there was only the sound of the ocean lapping at the beach. The dinosaur was dead, she was certain of that. So what had got Jane spooked so badly?

"It came from the ocean. I recognized it immediately. Somehow, the lagoon must be linked to the ocean by subterranean tunnels or something. I'm telling you that it crawled out of the ocean. It can walk on land. Don't you see? The lagoon can't hold it in. It's free, it's all around us. I thought you knew this? I thought you'd killed it?"

"You must be mistaken, Jane. It couldn't have been. You're saying you saw it on the beach? That thing from the lagoon?"

"I *saw* it. When I was at the lagoon, I saw its head, and when the monster climbed out of the ocean, I knew it was the same one."

Phoenix looked around frantically, still not seeing what Jane had spotted. Perhaps she had it wrong? Maybe she was having flashbacks and imagining it all. It wouldn't be the first time that Phoenix had seen someone replay events over in their head after going through a stressful near-death experience.

"Jane, we killed the dinosaur that stalked the jungle. You know, the one that looked like a T-rex. The one in the lagoon is trapped there. You must be wrong. The water in the lagoon is fresh. We drank it. If that water was fresh, then whatever monster lived in it couldn't survive at sea. It wouldn't be able to live in saltwater as well, right?"

Jane's bottom lip began to tremble and her eyes filled with water. "Crocodiles can survive in both. Everyone thinks they live in saltwater only, but it's not true. And this was far bigger and more powerful than any croc I've ever seen. Don't you see? It's here. It's not going to let us leave."

Phoenix looked at Karl swimming in the ocean. She saw Max walking along the beach. Suddenly, she felt sick. They weren't safe. Not even close. If Jane was right, then they had miscalculated

"Max, stop," said Phoenix. Yet as he began to run, she noticed the monster's attention drawn away from Karl. Its green eyes flickered and swiveled to look at Max. Perhaps the movement on the beach had done enough to draw it away from Karl. Max's cowardice may just be enough to save him.

Phoenix waded into the crystal-clear water up to her waist. Karl was half-swimming, half-running over the coral. She could see panic etched on his face and fear in his eyes.

"Come on, Karl, you can make it." She urged him on, beckoning him to her.

The dinosaur thrashed its tail around, sending huge waves toward the beach and then it lunged. Phoenix thought it was going to charge right at her, for Max and Jane, yet it changed direction and opened its jaws. Its jaws moved quickly, scooping up sea water, dead coral, and Karl. He tumbled over and over as the monster raised up its head, and Phoenix screamed with rage and frustration as it snapped its jaws shut. A huge wall of water fell from between its teeth. She heard Karl call out once, call her name, and then he was gone.

For a moment, she heard nothing. Max was gone, back to Jane. The dinosaur was swallowing Karl and looking at her silently. There were no more chances, no more options for Karl. He was dead. Phoenix was all that was left of her unit. She turned slowly and placed one foot in front of the other, the sea water clutching at her, trying to stop her from leaving. She reached the dry sand without thinking about what she would do next. Without Karl, it felt like she was nobody. Who was she without her men, without him? With her back to the beast, she looked and saw Max and Jane fighting. They were arguing over something, pushing and shoving like schoolchildren, but it all played out in her head like a silent movie. Even though she was back on the beach, the water was swelling up around her ankles. It was like a tsunami, pushing her forward, charging up the beach toward the jungle. Phoenix couldn't think anymore, couldn't think what to do next. What was there to do? She had nothing left. She was on her last legs and felt empty inside. It had all come to nothing.

"No!"

Jane's cries snapped Phoenix out of her shock. Max was pulling at something in Jane's hands. He was pulling at the machete, trying to get it off her. Phoenix saw Jane shove Max away and he tripped over, hitting his head on a small rock as he lay spread out on the beach. Phoenix felt cold suddenly as the sunlight disappeared and she knew what was next. She glanced over her shoulder, seeing the massive dinosaur close behind. It was ambling over the coral to her, its huge teeth dripping with saltwater and blood. The knowledge that she was about to die didn't come as any great shock or discomfort. It was how it should be. She had led her unit into battle and failed them all. They were dead. She was powerless now, unable to stop the inevitable.

Phoenix stopped halfway up the beach and closed her eyes. It was over. The machete hung limp in her hands. There was no fight left. Karl's death had made sure of that. A low rumble washed over her, a guttural sound that made her flesh crawl. She could feel the monster's breath warm her back.

She had lost.

CHAPTER 16

Phoenix grabbed Jane's hand. It was cold and limp. "Jane, *move*. We have to get away from here."

Jane stood like a statue, her eyes lost in a world of her own making.

"Jane, come on!" Phoenix shoved her and Jane followed as if she were a robot, her legs moving stiffly and reluctantly. Phoenix didn't care if Jane was in shock. They had no choice now but to abandon the rendezvous with Freddy. They had to abandon the beach and perhaps any chance of getting off the island forever.

Tears began to well in Phoenix's eyes. It wasn't the prospect of never getting home or the thought of being killed by the dinosaur, eaten alive. It was the knowledge that no matter what she did, Karl was dead. He was gone. Phoenix dragged Jane along, listening to the monster crawling along the island behind her. She didn't know where she was going, where to run to, but she had to get it away from Freddy. He at least could be saved. If he arrived in time to see that thing, he might even be able to raise the alert.

Phoenix ran along the beach with Jane, just hoping to live for one more day. It had been Jane who had brought her out of her stupor. Losing Karl was the final blow, the last thing she thought she could handle. Yet somehow Jane had made her see that there was still something she had to do. It was the fight with Max that had spurred her on. When Max had fallen, he had hit his head badly, enough to knock him unconscious. Jane had looked at Phoenix with disbelief. She had no idea what to do. The dinosaur that had killed Karl was almost on them. Phoenix had seen something in Jane then, something real and alive. She couldn't give up on her, this young girl who had survived for so long on her own.

Phoenix had sprinted out from underneath the grasping jaws of the monster and grabbed Jane. The monster had paused, giving Phoenix a chance. Jane had insisted on tending to Max, on trying to bring him around or carry him, but they had only seconds to decide. That was when Phoenix had told Jane they had to leave him. He had made his own bed. If he hadn't been so busy trying to force Jane into giving up the machete, he could have saved himself. There would've been time for everyone to get inland or find somewhere to hide. As it was, they were forced to leave Max behind. Jane had looked up into the monster's eyes and retreated into herself, and so Phoenix had been forced to drag her along by the hand.

A snapping sound caused Phoenix to turn and look back. She saw the dinosaur stood over Max. The creature's long body filled the beach and its tail crashed into the jungle, knocking down trees that had stood for years. She saw the dinosaur's jaws reach down and nudge Max. It was testing him, trying to find out if he was worth eating. The snapping noise was the sound of its jaws smashing together. She knew they could crush anything. They were designed for mincing bone, meat and tissue. There was no wonder the island was deserted. The local chief may have known what really lived on this island and created a story about it being an ancestral home, strictly off limits, to keep his people safe. The monsters had probably made short work of whatever animal life had once lived here: pigs, fowl, parrots, all decimated. Fish had to be a large part of their diet, perhaps even the odd inquisitive local who got too close. The thing hovering above Max did resemble a crocodile, but there was something more primitive about it. Now that it was out of the water, Phoenix appreciated its true size: it had to be eighty feet long and fifty feet high. It was undeniably another dinosaur.

Max rolled over and she saw him move an arm. Phoenix refused to feel guilty about it. She hoped he would stay unconscious. That might have saved him, but he was waking up now. The monster nudged his body again and Max sat upright. Phoenix saw his eyes widen in terror as the dinosaur leered over him. Suddenly, Max was on his feet and running, a thin line of blood dribbling down the side of his head from where he had fallen.

"Keep running, Jane," ordered Phoenix. "Keep going."

They found themselves running onto rocks and had to jump over several large rock-pools. The tide was coming in. Phoenix heard a cry and firmly held Jane's hand.

"Wait," said Jane as she pulled up. "I have to… I have to see this."

Phoenix glared at Jane. "We should keep going, Jane."

But Jane refused to move. Her eyes drifted back to the beach. The monster was chasing after Max. Phoenix saw him running toward them, tears streaming down his bloodied face. The monster could have caught him easily, snapped him up in its jaws in an instant, so why was it just following him? Was it just using him to lure them back?

"It's playing with him," said Jane in a monotone voice. "Like a—"

"Like a *cat*," said Phoenix. She had been thinking the same thing. "Jane, I really think we should move." Phoenix looked around. The rocks they were climbing were slippery and dangerous. Their progress would be slowed considerably by going over them, yet getting back to the beach or jungle was impossible. The monster would be able to get to them long before they reached the cover of the trees. "We don't have time to—"

Jane gasped as the monster lunged for Max. It knocked him off his feet with a glancing blow from its closed jaws. Max's body flew several yards through the air before hitting the ground. The wet sand was solid and he cried out in pain.

"*Wait*," said Jane again.

Phoenix watched Max try to get to his feet. His left arm hung limply by his side and she suspected it was broken. Agony was etched all over his face and as he struggled to get up the monster approached. Despite its size, it was agile and it jerked forward, latching its jaws around his midriff. Max screamed in pain as he was slowly lifted into the air.

"Jesus," whispered Phoenix. The guilt at leaving Max behind threatened to resurface so she thought of Karl. She remembered how Max had led them to this, tricked them and led to the deaths of her unit. No, she wasn't going to let his death be on her. He had brought this on himself.

The monster kept hold of Max and then smashed his body against the ground. Max yelled out in pain once more as the monster lifted him back up. Max's body was shattered. Phoenix could see blood dripping from his eyes and ears, and both his legs were twisted at unnatural angles. His white hair was matted with blood, and as he coughed, more blood spilled over his lips. The monster raised him high into the air and then slammed him back down onto the hard ground. Max didn't yell anymore.

Phoenix saw his body go limp. The monster dragged Max across the sand and then dropped him. The hideous creature's head turned to her and she saw its yellow eyes look at her and Jane. Was it gloating? Was it showing off, proving who was boss? Or was she just imagining it, projecting human thoughts onto a primitive animal that thought of nothing except eating and sleeping? She had no idea what sort of brain process the thing had, or if it had any idea what it was doing. It seemed to be toying with Max's body, as if deciding whether it was just a plaything or food.

With a movement that was so quick she almost missed it, the monster grabbed Max in its jaws, flipped him up into the air, and then swallowed him. His body was obliterated in the monster's powerful jaws, crushed to nothing, and then he was gone. Phoenix didn't feel any relief that Max was dead. She didn't think she cared anymore about what happened to him. He was just another name she was going to have to add to the long list of the dead when she got back home.

Home.

Phoenix turned to Jane. "Think we can go now?"

"I wanted to make sure. That bastard didn't come here for me. He would've let me die. All he wanted was the probe and the rocks."

Phoenix nodded. The sun was setting and Freddy would be here any time. A plan was forming in her mind. It was beyond dangerous, but there was little option. They could spend the rest of their lives playing hide and seek on the desolate island with the monster or they could try to find a way home. The only way off the island was Freddy's boat. She had to find a way to make it work.

Jane stepped up onto a rock and shielded her eyes from the setting sun. "It's over now. Max can rot in hell."

"I'm with you on that one, Jane." Phoenix watched the monster carefully. It was relishing the satisfaction that Max's body had provided for its belly. The dinosaur remained motionless for the moment. She had no doubt it wouldn't be long before it came for them. It had their scent now. It had a taste for human blood. Karl and Max had given it an appetite and next on the menu were her and Jane. "Give me your machete."

"Why?" Jane held it to her chest. "That's what Max said. You thinking of running out on me too?"

Phoenix had to admire Jane. Her strength was apparent, although it came and went. Sometimes she slipped back into lethargy or shock, probably because her body was now so weak. But the real Jane was a strong woman, a woman who deserved to live. "I've got an idea. It might just be the only way we can get to that boat. It's coming, Jane. It's coming right now, and if we miss it, there won't be another one. Trust me, I'm not like him. I'm not going to leave you."

Phoenix held out her hand and Jane offered her the machete. As Phoenix took it, she looked back at the monster. It took a step toward them and Phoenix looked back at Jane. "These rocks are going to save us, Jane. I'm going to wait right here for it." There was a small alcove to her right, dripping with seaweed. "You keep climbing over these rocks. You'll be down the other side before it can catch up with you. When you get to the other side, swim around it. Swim back to where we came from and find Freddy."

"Are you crazy? I'm not going to swim anywhere with that thing after us. And what about you? You're just going to hide and let me risk my ass?"

"No. I told you I have a plan. We're going to bait it. Give ourselves a chance."

"Let me guess, I'm the bait?"

"Sorry, Jane, but that fucker has a taste for us now. It will follow you, yes, but the second it gets up on these rocks, it will be forced to slow down. That's when I'm going to unleash fucking hell on that bastard. These two machetes should be enough. I'll cut its throat and carve out its eyes. Trust me. You'll have plenty of time to get around the rocks and back to the beach."

"I don't know. Shouldn't we just…?"

The dinosaur roared and charged. The tremors of its guttural roar sent vibrations through the ground and Phoenix scampered back into the alcove. Her feet splashed through a shallow rock-pool and she saw a crab scuttle away as she disturbed the water.

"Go, Jane, go!"

Jane hesitated for a moment, then turned and ran. She darted as quickly as she could up and over the rocks, and then was gone. Phoenix felt cold salty water drip down her back as she huddled back under the rock. The sun evidently never made it this far and the air was cool. The two machetes weighed heavily in her hands and Phoenix held onto them firmly. Her fingers coiled around the grips and she waited for the beast to appear. It would come right over her. She could feel it coming, feel its heavy body crashing over the rocks close by. It was chasing them and it wouldn't stop unless she could force it to. She *had* to make this work. She had been up close and personal with a dinosaur before. The one that resembled a T-rex in the jungle had tossed her around and she had scarcely made it out alive. Yet she had fought it off and won. She had to do it again. It was a different beast, but it was the same situation. It was kill or be killed. It was an animal, nothing more, nothing less. It had a beating heart, and if she could stop that, she could do anything. The stench of meat and blood stung her nostrils and she knew it was close. She gritted her teeth and prepared to run out of the cave. She wasn't afraid. She had a purpose and a job to do. She had a family to get home to. She had Jane to think of. If she failed then Jane would surely die, perhaps Freddy too. Nobody would know what happened here on this forgotten island. Karl didn't deserve that.

Phoenix stared out at a pool a few feet away. The shallow water rippled as the monster got closer. Phoenix felt the muscles in her legs screaming with pain and she looked down at the blood seeping from her wounds. There was nothing she could do about them now. She had to do this. She had to do it for her unit, for Jane, for Karl; for herself.

The dinosaur's jaws appeared first, reflected in the pool. Then she saw it. The monster was clambering over the rocks right above her. It was following Jane just as planned. The monster's lower jaw slowly emerged right above her like the hull of a boat, dribbling with bloody saliva. The skin was yellow and wrinkly, yet rough and covered in barnacles. As more of the monster appeared, she saw it plant one stout leg down right in front of her. The rock trembled beneath its weight and then Phoenix saw its neck. Skin sagged and shimmered in the low light, and she knew this was it. This was what she had to do. She had to strike whilst she had the chance.

Phoenix quickly got to her feet and ran from the cave. She screamed and lunged for the beast before it could move away. Whirling the two machetes above her head, she sliced through the skin, stabbing the sharp blades over and over into the monster's throat. A fountain of warm blood washed down over Phoenix and she raged as she slashed at the monster. Fire rained down over her, drenching her in sticky, foul gore.

"Fucking die!" she yelled as the monster reared up. She heard it bellow and then its jaws slammed down, threatening to squash her like a bug on the rocks.

Phoenix rolled away, grasping the machetes. Her whole body was covered in blood and gore. She suspected that some of what had swamped her was from Max. Pieces of bone and flesh slid down her aching body. She wiped her eyes and saw the monster rear up again. She ran to it, slamming the machetes' blades into its leg, using them like icepicks to climb up the beast. Every time she sliced one of the blades through its skin, she could feel its pain. The monster tried to buck her off, twisting around and around, but she held on. It was stuck atop the rocky outcrop, unable to quickly turn in either direction.

"Not this time, you bastard." Phoenix reached the top of the beast and straddled it. The machetes were buried deep within its body, wedged between its scales. "You like that?"

Phoenix plucked one of the blades out and put it between her teeth. The monster's blood, coppery and warm, filled her mouth, but she ignored it. She put her hands onto the monster's scales and crawled forward to its head. It was difficult holding on, but she was determined, desperate; she held on as the monster began to crawl back from where it had come, back to the beach. From the top of the monster, Phoenix saw Jane swimming in the water. She was almost back to the beach. The monster roared and Phoenix' body shuddered. The monster was heading back for the ocean, back to where it knew it was safe. It was trying to escape.

"You're not getting away that easy," said Phoenix as she took the machete from her mouth. She knew that if she let it get back to the water then it would be gone. She wouldn't be able to hold on. She had to finish it whilst she had it. This was their last chance.

Phoenix screamed and gripped the machete with both hands. She used her knees to hold onto the beast as she plunged it down, forcing the long blade right through the thick scales and skin into the creature's head. It roared in pain, letting out a sound that rippled over the ocean and sent pain soaring around Phoenix' head. The dinosaur charged forward, thrashing around as the blade stuck in its head. Phoenix tried to hold on, but the monster was weaving across the beach now and riding it was like trying to sit atop a bucking bronco during an earthquake. Her hands slid off the machete and she felt herself falling, slipping down the dinosaur's flank. Suddenly, she had lost contact with it altogether and she hurtled down toward the ground. The beach rushed up to meet her, and Phoenix slammed into it with such force that it knocked the breath out of her.

Phoenix lay on the hard sand, seaweed and shells scattered around her, unable to move. Her shoulder had popped out again, and she could barely keep her eyes open as she painfully tried to suck air into her lungs. She saw the dinosaur reach the edge of the ocean and then it slumped down to the ground. Its legs folded underneath it and its huge body hit the beach sending shuddering vibrations through Phoenix as she lay there. Sandflies bit her skin and she watched the dinosaur carefully. Was it finally dead? She tried to see if it was still breathing, but she couldn't tell. Its head was in the shallow water and it wasn't moving.

Phoenix coughed and blood trickled over her lips. The pain in her shoulder had spread to the rest of her body and it felt like someone had rammed a jagged knife through her chest. Phoenix tried to sit up, to look for Jane, to check that the dinosaur was dead, but her body refused to listen to her brain. It hurt too much. It hurt to keep her eyes open. Her head lifted only a few inches off the sand and then fell back down. The warm Pacific water began to wash up the beach, colored red, tainted with the dinosaur's blood. Phoenix closed her eyes. The sun was setting. Jane would find Freddy. The creature was dead. It was over. Phoenix let the welcome blackness envelope her. She would just lie here for a moment while the sun warmed her aching body. She just needed to rest for a minute, perhaps two. It hurt too much to do anything else. At least the dinosaur was dead. She had done it. She had killed two dinosaurs in one day.

And with that satisfying thought, Phoenix closed her eyes and slipped into unconsciousness.

CHAPTER 17

As the sun disappeared over the island's peak, Freddy turned off the boat's engine. They should have been back by now. They *should* be on the boat headed home. Yet the beach where he had dropped them was deserted, utterly devoid of life. Even the ocean was quiet, lapping gently at the sides of his boat. He scanned the trees looking for them, looking for an indication that they were on their way, perhaps just struggling to get through the undergrowth, but there was nothing. He listened intently, hoping to hear voices, cries for help or the sound of guns even, but still nothing. He waited until the sun sank almost out of sight and the island's shadow grew as dark as his mood. The sky began to turn from navy blue to black and the stars began to shine. Freddy began to realize that they might not be coming back at all. Something bad had happened here. He couldn't understand what: Phoenix and her men were well armed, prepared, and knew that they had to be back before sundown. What could possibly have stopped them all? There was nothing on the island but ghosts. He knew that the island was uninhabited. The most dangerous animal that they could meet was a scorpion or a wild hog, certainly nothing capable of stopping an entire unit of men armed with guns and machetes.

Freddy stirred the engine back into life. He had very few choices. There were three options open to him, none of which felt very satisfactory. The first one was to get out of the boat, go onto the island and look for them, despite his reservations about stepping on sacred land. The island was a big place, and realistically, he didn't hold much hope of finding them. He would have to cover a lot of ground in the dark and on his own. He had no more knowledge of the island and its interior than they did. It seemed futile to wander about in the dark, armed with nothing but a winning smile. The second choice was to take the boat around the island. It was possible that the unit had got themselves lost. It was certainly believable that they had ended up back on the wrong beach and been unable to find a path to the right one. Just because they had missed the rendezvous with him didn't necessarily mean something untoward had happened to them. He wanted to believe that. He wanted to find them just around the corner waiting patiently on another beach, hopefully with the three missing people they had come for. He truly thought that if he took the boat around the island and kept close to shore, he might find them. They would hear the sound of his engine as there was nothing else to hear, nothing to block it out at all, and all it would cost him was another hour or two of time. In the dark though he was going to need to be very careful not to breach or hit the shallow coral. If he miscalculated his distance from the shore, the horrible reality was that he would hit some rocks and then everyone was finished, including him. If the boat went, then so did their chance of getting home. Nobody knew where he was. He hadn't told the chief, his family or any friends about the excursion to the forbidden island. That meant the third and final option presented him with a dilemma. Choosing the third option meant going against his own will, against everything he stood for. He was responsible for these people. He had brought them here, left them with a smile, a wave and a promise to return.

He kept watching the beach hoping to see Phoenix step out of the grass and call to him. He watched through the setting darkness carefully, but of course, he saw nothing. The third option was really the most practical one: he had to leave.

Freddy pulled the boat out of the small inlet slowly. He steered the boat around to the north where he knew there were other small beaches. It wouldn't hurt to look, just in case they had accidentally made their way to the wrong place. Still, he was nervous and spent half of his time watching the shallow ocean for rocks. Keeping a constant watch on the island's shore was impossible. He would sail right past them if he wasn't careful.

Remembering Phoenix made Freddy smile. He admired her, how she managed to control all those men and make them work for her. It couldn't be easy, leading people into unknown territory. For all he knew, she had a husband and children back in America. He really knew very little about her or her unit. All he had been told was that he would be taking a small band of soldiers to the island to look for the three missing people he had taken a few days previously. He hadn't realized one of them would be a woman.

Freddy watched the jungle carefully as the boat rounded a small bay. Perhaps he should have stayed. If something had gone wrong, they would have been able to signal him. If they had needed to get away, he would've been right there. He chastised himself for being such a coward. In truth, he feared the chief finding out that he was helping them. The island was a sacred place, off limits to everyone, even the chief. He had returned home and spent the day fishing, doing a little bookkeeping in between taking care of his nieces. He had kept himself busy when he should have been looking out for the Americans. What happened to them was on him. He knew he couldn't leave, not yet. He had to at least search for them thoroughly. In the gloom of night, he couldn't see that the island had changed. It looked the same as when he had left it that morning. So, where were they? What had the island done to cause them such a problem that they couldn't return to him as planned?

There was an outcrop of rocks and then a larger beach that stretched for at least half a mile. The beach was empty and he watched the trees for any sign of a disturbance. If Phoenix was late and still leading her men back through the jungle, then any birds nestling in the high branches of the trees would be unsettled. But nothing flew into the air. Nothing crawled out of the grass flanking the edges of the beach and nobody called out to him to stop.

The third option was fast becoming the only choice. The faint dim sunlight over the horizon was casting barely any light now, creating a red glow in the distance. The moon was low behind him and not yet bright enough to light the island. He had brought these people here and now they were lost. Freddy knew he had to go home. He wasn't going to find them. If he stayed any longer, he would be stranded himself. It was almost time to leave. He would give them a few more minutes, until the sun disappeared for the day, and then he would have to go home. He had responsibilities there too, to his family, and he couldn't spend the night out here alone.

As Freddy turned the boat away from shore, something caught his eye. There was movement at the furthest end of the beach. Something was moving in the darkness, although he couldn't be sure what it was. A natural jetty headed out to sea made up of large volcanic rocks. It extended out into the ocean about thirty feet. At its tip, where the rocks disappeared under the water, something was moving. It could be Phoenix or one of her men, and Freddy felt excited. Had they simply got lost after all? He throttled up the engine and headed straight for the outcrop of rocks. He kept his eyes firmly on the moving shape and waited for it to get clearer. Quickly, it became apparent it was one of them. Whether it was Phoenix or not he wasn't sure, but it was a start. All thoughts of leaving were long gone. He felt foolish for thinking the worst. They had simply taken a wrong turn and ended up on the wrong beach. He smiled with relief. It was time to go home.

"I'm coming!" shouted Freddy, hoping they would hear his voice above the engine. "Stay there, stay there."

As he got closer to the rocks, the faint moonlight and last droplets of sunlight illuminated the lone figure, and Freddy recognized Phoenix.

"Phoenix? Hold on!" Freddy yelled and felt his heart racing. She was waving to him. She was alone which was worrying, but she was alive. Maybe she had got separated from her unit, or perhaps her men were just waiting under cover of the jungle. Either way, Freddy was pleased he wasn't going home alone. He had thought about telling the chief what he had done, and was pleased that was a conversation he no longer had to have. The consequences of bringing more people to the island would have been severe. Now, with Phoenix back, he felt relief. They had simply got lost. He imagined the rest of her unit waiting on the beach, sitting around telling jokes with the people they had rescued. It was going to be okay. Freddy exhaled, relieved. It was going to be okay.

He heard her voice only when he was much closer. Over the rumble of the boat's engine, he had heard only his own thoughts. She was still waving at him, one arm high above her head, and as he got closer, he began to make out her face. Her face was troubled. There was a nasty gash above one eye and she was covered in dirt and sand. She looked beat up. He had to get her off that outcrop quickly. He slowed the engine down and let the boat drift the last few feet.

"Phoenix, I'm sorry, I thought I had lost you. Are you…?"

She continued waving at him and then he finally heard her, finally hearing what she had been saying to him all the time. "Get out of here, Freddy. Get away. Just leave!"

"What? I'm going to take you home. Don't worry, whatever's happened, I can help you." The boat was barely twenty feet from her now and he could see pain etched over her face. It made no sense. Why was she telling him to leave? He was right when he thought something bad had happened, but quite what he had no idea. For her to tell him to leave made him think that one of her men had done something, perhaps gone insane and taken out the others? Was she trying to protect him from her own unit? What if there had been some sort of mutiny and they had hurt her?

"Stay there, I'll get you, Phoenix." Freddy steered the boat closer. "Just stay there, okay?"

He could see Phoenix begin crying. She collapsed to her knees and continued waving at him. Her other arm hung by her side motionless. She wasn't beckoning him to her but trying to tell him to go back.

"Freddy, get the fuck out of here, for your own sake."

Through the gasps and sobs, he heard her, but he didn't understand.

"Look, it'll be okay. Just try to relax and I'll—"

There was a bump on the hull of his boat and Freddy anxiously looked down. He expected to see a rock sticking through the steel and water leaking onto the boat, but there was nothing there, just the gangplank and his supplies. He had been lucky. He knew he must be getting closer to the rocks now and it was just a fluke that he hadn't torn a hole in the underside of the boat. He had to be more careful and not rush.

"Wait, I've got to figure out how to get you." Freddy wondered if she would be able to swim. He wasn't going to be able to get the boat right up to her. Given her current state, he didn't think she had the energy to swim the twenty feet to the boat. The best option was the beach. He would be able to collect her there. "Phoenix, can you get back to the beach? The water is too shallow. I can't get close enough to—"

Another bump under the boat knocked Freddy off his feet. He fell backward and grabbed hold of the gangplank. Yet despite a small splash of water, he was still dry. The boat was still intact. That was twice he had got lucky. He had narrowly missed being thrown overboard by whatever the boat had hit. The volcanic rocks were difficult to navigate in daylight, and in the gloom of the late evening, he was worried that another strike might put a hole right through the hull.

"There's something in the water. You need to get out of here, *right now*."

Freddy heard Phoenix shout and he managed to get to his feet as the boat swayed and rocked. The ocean was quiet and still, so why was the boat moving around so much? "Phoenix? What are you talking about? It's the rocks. I need to—"

"Freddy, listen to me," pleaded Phoenix. "I thought it was dead. I thought I'd killed it. But it was just another trick. When I came around, it was gone. Don't you see? It's in the water. You need to get the fuck away from me. It's not the rocks. Jane—"

The skin on his arms shivered and Freddy saw it just before his world turned upside down. A creature was rising out of the sea, approaching quickly to his port side. It was huge, magnificent, like nothing he had ever seen before. This was neither a shark nor a whale. This was something else, something new—or old. As the monster's jaws opened and threatened to swallow the boat whole, Freddy remembered tales of leviathans that his tribe used to fight. They were just stories passed down through the generations. He hadn't believed any of them until now. The beast racing toward him was beyond what those tales had described. It had elongated jaws and yellow eyes, a tail that had to be fifty feet long, and terrifying teeth that would rip both him and his boat apart in seconds.

Freddy screamed as the monster rose up out of the water. Its body was as large as an airplane and it was like a jumbo jet flying up out of the water. The monster made a roaring sound too, not dissimilar to the noise of a jet taking off at full speed. The thing's skin was glistening wet and its head was the size of his home. He felt like laughing, but Freddy was too scared. It was absurd, but it was real, so real he could smell the musty, salty stench oozing from its pores. Phoenix had tried to warn him, but he hadn't listened. Now he understood that she wasn't waving at him to come and get her, but for him to get away. She had tried to warn him, to save him, but it was too late. She hadn't got lost or had a problem with her unit. The problem was the monster. It didn't occur to Freddy that it might actually be a dinosaur.

Freddy caught sight of the creature's eyes. It had two massive yellow eyes on either side of its head and its black pupils were looking right at him. Freddy felt his bladder weaken as he looked upon its teeth. Even in the dim light, he could see it had a mouth full of sharp teeth that would snap him in half before he even knew what was happening. There had to be a hundred razor sharp teeth baring down on him. This thing had hunted him, probably followed him for a while before taking its chance. Had it waited until he was in shallow water? The monster was terrifying, roaring as it sprang out of the water and descended upon Freddy and his little boat.

There was only a second before he would be hit, and there was no way of navigating the boat out of the creature's path. His engine was simply not large enough to power him out of the way. Freddy knew it was over. He tried to jump out of the boat before the impact, but there was not enough time. In the split second that it took him to jump, he hoped that he might be able to swim to the rocks, to Phoenix, but the monster crashed down onto the boat, smashing it instantly into pieces. Freddy felt the brute force of the thing's lower jaw smash into him and then he was under water. Pieces of his boat were swirling around him in the chaos and bubbles of air swarmed and circled around him. Freddy was tossed around roughly in the churning water as the monster destroyed the boat. He gasped and tried to swim for the surface, but the water was throwing him around like a fish in a hurricane.

"Freddy?" Phoenix clutched her ribs as she screamed his name. Her heart raced like a jackhammer. "Freddy!"

The boat was destroyed. The dinosaur had fooled her and won. When she had woken up on the beach, it had taken her a moment to understand what had happened. Getting to her feet, she had found a trail of blood leading into the ocean. It had survived. It had retreated back into the water where it could recuperate and lick its wounds. The dinosaur had left her, perhaps thinking she was dead too. Wandering around the beach, she had wondered for a while if maybe she was dead. The sun had begun to set and she was weak. She had spent some time on her knees praying, a little time sobbing, and a little time angrily shouting and pleading in desperation for someone to come and get her. Of course, it had all been futile. She had even gone back into the jungle for a while, unable to believe she was stranded and alone once more. Once dusk settled over the island, the jungle had become too cold and she wandered back out to the beach, unsure what to do next. She listened for the boat, for Freddy, for any sign he was coming. And then she had found Jane.

Her body had washed up on a small inlet, and if Phoenix hadn't found her when she had, then Jane would probably have died from exposure. She was unconscious but alive. Phoenix had dragged her up the beach, up toward the jungle where she had found some dry leaves and covered Jane up to try to get her warm. The woman was barely breathing. Phoenix had assumed she was dead, drowned, or eaten, yet somehow, she had escaped the monster. There were bruises on her arms and a nasty cut on the back of her head, but she was alive. Phoenix had done what she could for her and made her comfortable, and then left her to sleep. Sanity returned to Phoenix once she'd found Jane, and remembering the boat had forced her back onto the beaches. It was only as the sun was setting that she finally heard an engine.

"Freddy, no." Phoenix watched the remains of the boat slip beneath the surface. The dinosaur had annihilated it beyond repair. There was nothing to salvage. With the wreckage of the boat slipping beneath the ocean, Phoenix's hopes of rescue also receded. There was no way back now. Freddy was gone. Phoenix watched the dinosaur slink away, its massive tail pushing it over the coral and around the inlet. Was it going out to sea or back to the lagoon? It didn't matter anymore. It hadn't even bothered to finish her off. Somehow, it knew that by destroying the boat it had destroyed any chance she had of getting off the island. Freddy was dead, either drowned or swallowed up by the dinosaur.

Phoenix wished she had been quicker. When she'd heard the engine, she had raced out onto the rocky outcrop as far as she dared, hoping to warn him away. She hoped she might be able to make him understand, but she'd been too slow. Phoenix began to trudge back over the rocks to the beach. What was she going to tell Jane? Was Jane even still alive? Phoenix slowly walked over the rocks and picked her way down to the beach. The hard sand soon turned soft and then she was back with Jane who was nestled underneath a large tree. She was awake and watched as Phoenix sank down to the ground and curled up beside her.

"How are you doing?" Phoenix felt Jane's forehead. She was burning up, but at least she was breathing. Phoenix felt deflated. What was the point in rescuing Jane only to become stranded herself? "You feel up to walking? We should probably find somewhere more sheltered for the night."

"Has it gone?" asked Jane quietly. She coughed and looked at Phoenix. "I saw it. I woke up when that boat came. You couldn't have done anything. There was no way to warn him. Was it Freddy? I don't suppose he—"

"No, I don't think so." Phoenix looked at the still ocean. There was a crescent moon in the distance that broke up over the coral. Her body needed sleep. She had nothing left to offer. She had no energy and certainly no time to waste on giving Jane false hope. There was no rescue coming. They had blown it. "The dinosaur's gone and so has our ride home. We're stuck here." Now that the dinosaur was gone, it seemed eerily quiet on the island. Everything had gone back to the way it was, so quiet and still. It was time to face reality. "We're going to die here," said Phoenix softly.

Jane sighed. "Fuck."

As they sat in silence and watched the moon rise over the ocean, Phoenix heard a splashing noise. A seagull or something had probably found a crab. It came from the shallows. As she listened, she heard more splashing and then something loomed up out of the water. The thought that she might have to face the monster again so soon was pressing on her brain, so she was relieved to see what emerged from the ocean was just a man.

"What the...?"

Phoenix jumped to her feet and pulled Jane up.

"Who's there?"

The dark figure ambled up the beach toward them and only when she heard the man cough did she realize who it was.

"Freddy? Is that you?"

Phoenix and Jane went to him as he collapsed on the dark beach. His legs folded quickly and he fell on his back. Phoenix held his cold wet body and brushed the seaweed from his face.

"I thought you were dead. I thought—" Phoenix looked him over. Apart from being half drowned, he looked fine. There were no visible cuts or broken bones. It was a miracle he was still alive. Somewhere in the chaos, he must've found a way to get past the monster.

Freddy coughed up salt water. "Me... too."

Jane and Phoenix helped him to sit up. Freddy shook his head. "Just what... what the hell *was* that thing?"

Phoenix looked at Jane for answers.

"A throwback. A relic of a lost age." Jane shrugged. "A dinosaur."

Freddy took Phoenix' hand. "Is that what delayed you?"

"Yeah. That and... well, it's been a long day."

Freddy glanced around at the jungle. "Just you two?"

Phoenix nodded. She felt so weary. She wanted to get off the island so desperately. "It's just us. The others—" Phoenix shook her head.

"Will someone come for you, Freddy?" asked Jane. "Is there another boat? You told someone about the rescue operation, didn't you?"

Freddy cleared his throat. "I'm afraid it's just the three of us."

Phoenix felt like crying. She missed her family. "So, nobody knows we're here?"

Freddy rubbed his lips, wiping away the salty saliva. He had tasted enough of the ocean. He looked back at the jungle and said nothing. Then he slowly got to his feet and planted his hands on his hips.

"It won't be easy." His chest heaved as he got his breath back. "Not tonight, but I can do it in the morning."

"Do what?" Jane threw her hands up in the air. "Do *what*, Freddy? You just said that nobody knows where we are. Nobody is coming. We are so fucked."

Phoenix watched Freddy. Even in the darkness, she could see his eyes fixed firmly on the jungle. He was thinking about something, planning something. After being nearly eaten by a dinosaur and then drowned, he was already thinking about how to escape the island. He hadn't seen them die though, hadn't watched her unit suffer and die horribly. Did he understand just what they were up against?

"I can get it done if you help me," said Freddy. He looked at Jane and then Phoenix, his eyes glimmering under the moonlight, his wet body illuminated by the stars. The ocean rocked gently behind him and the world slept. "I can build a raft. We have plenty of wood to use and the vines are strong. I can use those to lash the wood together. It won't be pretty, but it'll work. I know these ocean currents. We can get home, to my home. From there, we can get in touch with your military."

"A raft? Do you think you can build something strong enough to get us away from here?" asked Jane.

Phoenix saw Jane's face light up. "And what about that monster?" Phoenix wanted so hard to believe in him, but her fight had gone. Most of it had left her body when she had bled all over the beach. "What if it finds us?"

Freddy licked his upper teeth and cocked his head to one side. "It's dark now. The monster must sleep sometime. We'll go then."

Phoenix couldn't help it. She genuinely smiled despite herself. "Careful, Freddy, you've almost got me believing you."

Jane clapped her hands together. "Well, *I* believe you. I'll do whatever I can to help. Freddy, this island is not what you thought. We really need to get out of here."

"I get that," replied Freddy. "What do you say, Phoenix? You want to get off this island?"

"You're damn right I do." Phoenix shivered. "We'll do it together. The three of us working together, right?"

"No problem," said Freddy. "I'm not beaten yet and neither are you. After what I just saw, I can't believe you two are still standing. I think you can do anything you want. We got this beat."

Phoenix looked at the ocean as a tear came to her eye. She wished Karl was at her side, but the best thing she could do for him now was to get home and make sure he was honored in the right way. She had something to believe in again. She knew the ocean crossing would be difficult, but it was possible. They didn't have to die on the island. They could go home. The nightmare would be over soon.

As Phoenix dreamt of home, a deafening roar shattered the silence. It soared across the jungle's rooftop, out across the island and smothered the Pacific Ocean. The ground started vibrating and the sand beneath Phoenix's feet shifted. It was as if she were back on the hillside when the dinosaur had attacked. She looked at Freddy and Jane as she heard movement nearby in the jungle.

"Run!"

THE END?

ACKNOWLEDGEMENTS

The Yasawa Islands are real and far more inviting than I can describe accurately in this novel. A visit will show you their natural beauty, both of the land and in the people. Happily, there are no dinosaurs. At least none that I know of…

Please check out the numerous quality novels Severed Press have also have produced at www.severedpress.com.

Also, consider leaving a review and pay a visit to my website www.russwatts.co or check out my other titles:
The Afflicted
The Grave
The Ocean King
Adrenal7n
Devouring the Dead
Devouring the Dead 2: Nemesis
Goliath
Hamsikker
Hamsikker 2
Hamsikker 3
Zombiekill

CHECK OUT OTHER GREAT DINOSAUR THRILLERS

LOST WORLD OF PATAGONIA
by Dane Hatchell

An earthquake opens a path to a land hidden for millions of years. Under the guise of finding cryptid animals, Ace Corporation sends Alex Klasse, a Cryptozoologist and university professor, his associates, and a band of mercenaries to explore the Lost World of Patagonia. The crew boards a nuclear powered All-Terrain Tracked Carrier and takes a harrowing ride into the unknown.

The expedition soon discovers prehistoric creatures still exist. But the dangers won't prevent a sub-team from leaving the group in search of rare jewels. Tensions run high as personalities clash, and man proves to be just as deadly as the dinosaurs that roam the countryside.

Lost World of Patagonia is a prehistoric thriller filled with murder, mayhem, and savage dinosaur action.

SAVAGE ISLAND
by Alan Spencer

Somewhere in the Atlantic Ocean, an uncharted island has been used for the illegal dumping of chemicals and pollutants for years by Globo Corp's. Private investigator Pierce Range will learn plenty about the evil conglomerate when Susan Branch, an environmentalist from The Green Project, hires him to join the expedition to save her kidnapped father from Globo Corp's evil hands.

Things go to hell in a hurry once the team reaches the island. The bloodthirsty dinosaurs and voracious cannibals are only the beginning of the fight for survival. Pierce must unlock the mysteries surrounding the toxic operation and somehow remain in one piece to complete the rescue mission.

Ratchet up the body count, because this mission will leave the killing floor soaked in blood and chewed up corpses. When the insane battle ends, will there by anybody left alive to survive Savage Island?

CHECK OUT OTHER GREAT DINOSAUR THRILLERS

THE VALLEY
by Rick Jones

In a dystopian future, a self-contained valley in Argentina serves as the 'far arena' for those convicted of a crime. Inside the Valley: carnivorous dinosaurs generated from preserved DNA. The goal: cross the Valley to get to the Gates of Freedom. The chance of survival: no one has ever completed the journey. Convicted of crimes with little or no merit, Ben Peyton and others must battle their way across fields filled with the world's deadliest apex predators in order to reach salvation. All the while the journey is caught on cameras and broadcast to the world as a reality show, the deaths and killings real, the macabre appetite of the audience needing to be satiated as Ben Peyton leads his team to escape not only from a legal system that's more interested in entertainment than in justice, but also from the predators of the Valley.

JURASSIC DEAD
by Rick Chesler & David Sakmyster

An Antarctic research team hoping to study microbial organisms in an underground lake discovers something far more amazing: perfectly preserved dinosaur corpses. After one thaws and wakes ravenously hungry, it becomes apparent that death, like life, will find a way.
Environmental activist Alex Ramirez, son of the expedition's paleontologist, came to Antarctica to defend the organisms from extinction, but soon learns that it is the human race that needs protecting.

CHECK OUT OTHER GREAT DINOSAUR THRILLERS

WRITTEN IN STONE
by David Rhodes

Charles Dawson is trapped 100 million years in the past. Trying to survive from day to day in a world of dinosaurs he devises a plan to change his fate. As he begins to write messages in the soft mud of a nearby stream, he can only hope they will be found by someone who can stop his time travel. Professor Ron Fontana and Professor Ray Taggit, scientists with opposing views, each discover the fossilized messages. While attempting to save Charles, Professor Fontana, his daughter Lauren and their friend Danny are forced to join Taggit and his group of mercenaries. Taggit does not intend to rescue Charles Dawson, but to force Dawson to travel back in time to gather samples for Taggit's fame and fortune. As the two groups jump through time they find they must work together to make it back alive as this fast-paced thriller climaxes at the very moment the age of dinosaurs is ending.

HARD TIME
by Alex Laybourne

Rookie officer Peter Malone and his heavily armed team are sent on a deadly mission to extract a dangerous criminal from a classified prison world. A Kruger Correctional facility where only the hardest, most vicious criminals are sent to fend for themselves, never to return.

But when the team come face to face with ancient beasts from a lost world, their mission is changed. The new objective: Survive.

www.ingramcontent.com/pod-product-compliance
Lightning Source LLC
Chambersburg PA
CBHW032008170626
46807CB00006B/2705